MW01491369

THE GENTLEMEN OF D-BLOCK 2

Chain Gang

SA'ID SALAAM

Urban Aesop Presents

Saidsalaam.com

Email: SaidmSalaam@gmail.com

Facebook: Free Said Salaam or Black Ink Publications

Cover design: Adriane Hall

Editor: Brandi Jordan

Chapter One

"*H*ey, my nigga JJ!" Rallo cheered as his co-defendant was brought down to the transport area of the Cobb County Jail. He had struck a good deal to snitch on Rallo but still had a year and a half to serve. "Where you been?"

"Rallo! What's good shawty! Mane these folks tripping! They had a playa on lockdown! Talmbout some, protective custody!" JJ reeled like it was a shock. It really wasn't a shock since he begged them not to put him back in population after snitching. The Rollers would have beat him in any dorm he was housed in. If they didn't the Riders would have gotten him. Or even the civilians since no one likes a snitch.

"P.C! Not a playa like you!" Rallo exclaimed. "What they give you?"

"Shit, I had to take a dime cuz my record fucked up! I woulda got a dub for recidivist if I ain't take the ten," he explained which explained why he snitched. Had he admitted to getting eighteen months that would have been proof of his cooperation as well. "We Gucci?"

"As a mug!" Rallo assured him and dapped him up. They ran through the now elaborate series of twist and turns that made up the Roller's handshake. They could remember all that but fractions were still a mystery to most. That would be the last time they got to use their hands before they were shackled. Hands cuffed to a waist chain and ankles cuffed.

The men shuffled into a van for the ride down the road. The ten men all watched their city fade in the windows as they headed south. Urban blight gave way to suburban sprawl. None of the men ventured too far from their blocks and hoods so they rode in silence and took it all in.

Anyone one of them could have been anything else had they grown up anywhere else other than the hood. Limited opportunities limited their vision beyond trapping or rapping. All ten would have a chance to try again in a few years once released. Unfortunately some would make this trip again and dream these same daydreams again. First they had to survive D-Block.

"Shit," one of the men moaned when they reached the prison. Something about the razor wire, concrete and guard towers made him realize the seriousness of his crimes. None of the dirty money was worth living behind those walls.

"Looks like a dungeon!" An older, white inmate moaned. The sight alone brought his inner bitch to the surface

"Shoulda thought about that when you was messing

with them kids Merle," another inmate who was familiar with his case grunted. Even JJ snarled at the man he shared space with in the protective custody dorm of the county jail. Snitches are low but child molesters are the lowest of the low. They deserved everything they had coming.

"Last stop gentlemen," one of the transport officers sighed as they pulled to a stop. They were among the first to arrive but a caravan of vans would be coming all day and all week. Most of the incoming inmates were coming from other prisons but county jails from every Georgia county was dropping off as well.

The inmates filed off the van and waited for the instant relief that comes from removal of the shackles. The unnatural feel of cold steel on ankles and wrist are in itself a punishment. Throughout history they had been enough to deter from crimes. One taste of cuffs set many a man and woman on the straight and narrow.

A false sense of security swept through the small group when the CERT team sergeant cordially greeted the transport officers. The short, stocky black man smiled and shook hands as he collected the files and signed the men over to custody of the chain gang. Then, went ice cold as he turned to face the new arrivals.

"On your faces!" Sergeant Quick shouted as the rest of his ten man team rushed from every angle. The few who were confused by his command learned the lesson the hard way when they were slammed on their faces. Two tried to buck and the beating that followed taught them a lesson the hard way.

"Ouch!" Warden Mays giggled as they watched from

the window. She had set aside a few minutes to watch when a particular few inmates made their grand appearance. This van contained the infamous Rallo 'Roller', the head of the Rollers. The gang had been raising hell all over the system. He could be the solution to her plans to get rich. They certainly had the muscle it took to run a drug ring behind the wall.

"Brown skin, short fro, on the left," Davis announced after matching him up to the file. He was one of the ones who had to be slammed on their faces but the only one who hopped up and fought back.

"Feisty. I like him," Mays nodded as Rallo was quickly tased and subdued. Once he came to his senses they resumed being processed into the prison.

They moved through the different sections and got hair cuts, shaved, and sized up for their uniforms. Once they passed through a delousing shower they were photographed while still wet and naked.

"Hole up! Let a nigga prime up!" Rallo joked and gave his dick a few pulls before he got his picture taken. He whipped up a nice semi erection but that's not what they were looking for. Still, he did have what they were after. The tattoos may have well have been hieroglyphics to most but they had someone there who spoke that.

"You, over there," an officer barked at Rallo and pointed off to the side.

"This must be the big dick section?" He joked and complied. The officer stared a hole through him and erased the smirk before checking out the next man. Rallo wasn't in the mood to go another round with the Cert team so he got dressed and shut up.

"Fuck wrong with you?" The same officer snapped at the child molester who had a full fledged hard on from seeing the other naked men.

"I'm sorry," he pouted as his body was photographed. Young boys were his main thing but booty is booty to a pervert. He didn't have any tattoos just yet but the day was still young. Someone was sure to claim him and write their name on him somewhere. Those like him get passed along, traded or sold and end up with half a phone book on their body.

Only one other inmate had gang tattoos besides Rallo so they were seated aside to talk to the gang task force officer. Rallo was identified by the tattoos he sported while the Spanish man was Spanish so he was a Mexican by default. Good thing he was actually Mexican since he would be linked with the gang.

The gang unit was headed by a thirty something black woman. It was hard to place a finger if she was pretty or not since she hid her features behind a mask of makeup, large eyelashes and weaves. She looked more like a man dressed as a woman except for the bodacious body. The old timers called it, 'finer than a muhfucka'.

"What set you claim?" Sergeant Pike asked even though she already knew. She just wanted to see if he was dumb enough to admit it.

"O.G. Roller Rallo, baby girl! I'm that Rallo!" He bragged and posed as she would be impressed. It was impressive to some young hoes in the hood but Sergeant Pike was more of a financial portfolio type of gal.

"Good, so now we know who to hold accountable," she nodded and pointed to the door. She had a busy day ahead of her since she had to make sure to balance the facility out with gang members. She had to sprinkle them amongst the civilians just right. Too many of one and not enough of another would upset the balance and start a war.

"Shoot I'm finna go crazy down here! First nigga try me, they getting it! On my mama!" A youth called Petey vowed as the van from Fulton county neared the prison. He was one of the few civilians on the van and was hyping himself up for the big leagues.

Trouble respected his decision not to get down with a gang and now it was time to live up to it. Lil-Zay opened his mouth to shut his since he had been yapping the whole two hour ride from the city. Trouble waved him off with a nod since they were almost there. He could live up to it or die about it real soon.

"Fuck it, I'm just finna be a moozlim!" Another man decided at the last moment. As if Islam is a last option if all else fails. This was his third bid so he knew what lay ahead. The chain gang is the land of predator and prey with nothing in between. He would just slide in the ranks of the Muslims until it was time to go home.

Trouble just shook his head once more since he grew up with a bunch of Muslims on the West side of Atlanta. Some were good, others were bad, but none made the decision as a bus pulled into a prison. It's a lot more to it than, 'fuck it, I'm finna be a Muslim'.

Trouble was a Rider for life but had plans for the rest of

his life that didn't include being a Rider. The hundred grand he left in the safe was a good start on a new life once he got out. Keeping his nose clean could cut five years off the ten and that's all that mattered.

"Aye, y'all niggas do what these niggas in black say do!" The transport officer in the passenger seat warned as they pulled. He was hood to his heart but just got a job at the jail before ending up in the jail.

"Facts cuz they keep a hard on for niggas from city!" The driver added. He was hood too and advised. "Do ya time and come the fuck back to ya family!"

All heads nodded since nothing much mattered. Trouble stifled a smile at the thought of little Trevor's little face. It translated into a smirk until the van pulled to a stop. They were quickly surrounded by the CERT team, pounding on the windows with their fist. The intimidation factor intimidated every except big mouth Petey.

"Fuck y'all niggas beating on the glass 'fo!" He shouted back. Both officers shook their heads, knowing what was coming.

"Hole up. Y'all sign for them first!" The passenger demanded so they couldn't be blamed for the injuries sure to follow. Sergeant Quick quickly scribbled his name before his officers snatched the doors open.

"Take the cuffs off and give me a head up!" Big mouth demanded as he was drug off the van. Today's lesson was don't talk shit with your hands cuffed to your side.

"Oh shit!" The rest of the men sang like a well rehearsed choir. The dense thuds of the kicks and punches only further made the point they were trying to make. They beat Petey like he stole something. He stole cars to get here so this was for that too. For all those hard working people who woke up to find their cars missing from their driveways.

"On your fa..." Was all Quick got to before the rest of the men hit the deck. Warden Davis nodded from the window when she matched Trouble to his file.

"Mr Clayton...*might get him some pussy*," Warden Mays said and thought as she looked at his picture. His smooth chocolate skin was dipped in handsome but the intelligence in his eyes made her plump vagina throb one good time.

"Drug charges. So he either he knows how to hustle or not," Davis wondered. He was a dope boy, but then again he was here which means he got caught. Either way he was officially on the radar as he went inside to be processed.

Trouble made it through the showers and photographs without being outed since he didn't have any ink. He was thinking long term when Ridell and most of the crew got their brand tatted on arms, chest, backs, necks and faces. He learned a lesson taught in business schools about the powers of branding.

Lil-Zay had the Riders ink on his arms, chest, back, neck and face. He and the two Rollers on board were pulled out to speak with the gang unit. Being tagged as a gang member would show as a red flag on their records. It could cost parole and Trouble was trying to get home.

"Missing one aren't we?" Sergeant Pike asked when her count came up one short. Her Intel had the intelligent Trevor 'Trouble' Clayton all over it. Men in prison were taking oaths in his and Ridell's name and Ridell was dead.

"That's all the ones with tats?" He said and began a double check she didn't have time for.

"Trevor Clayton. Send him in!" She said and turned. The command almost got lost when he looked down an locked in on all that ass shifting around in her khaki pants.

"Clayton, sarge need to see you," the officer repeated when he remembered what she said.

"That bitch fine! I think it's a bitch?" Lil-Zay cheered then wondered. He lived his entire life in a city where you need to check a birth certificate to certify that a woman was born that way. Only in Atlanta could a chick have big titties and a big dick.

"Whatever that means," Trouble laughed and went where he was pointed. He tapped on the open door and waited.

"Come. Sit. Name. Set?" Pike barked without looking up at the man seated before her. Trouble liked attention well enough to want some so he sat silently until he got some. It came with a dose of sarcasm. "Uh, your file doesn't say anything about a hearing impediment!"

"No ma'am, I hear just fine," he semi smiled but held off on the charm when he saw why Zay was confused. The heavy accessories were just like the fuck men back home wore to hide their masculinity. A split second later he recognized she was all woman. "That is my name on the paper. Trevor Clayton but, Ion know nothing about no set? Like tennis?"

"No not like tennis!" She snapped even if slightly amused. "Which set of the Riders? Whoo-Ride!"

"I ain't in no gang ma'am. The Riders are in my hood

so I grew up around them all. We..." He was saying as her thick lips twisted dubiously.

"Keep that same energy because I promise to hold you responsible for any and everything done by your gang," she vowed and closed his file. She moved on to the next file since more vans with more gang bangers were on the way.

Chapter Two

"Wake him up!" An officer barked as they pulled up to the prison.

"I'm not sleeping," Rabbit announced but didn't open his eyes yet. He had always kept them closed tightly when transferring since he didn't want to see stuff he couldn't have. Especially women.

The CERT team lost a little of their vigor by the time this van arrived. They banged a little less and shouted a little lower. The van load were all vets so no one needed to get jumped on to make a point. They were ushered inside the building and processed in.

Sergeant Pike interviewed him as well and made the same useless threat. Sure whatever the White boys did would come from him but what could they do about it. Many life flight helicopters and landed at many prisons just off of a nod of his head. This was the end of the road for the worst of the worst.

The days of whites being dominated, oppressed and

abused in Georgia prison came to an end. The black gangs made it easy for him to fight back since they were fractured into so many different groups. They were always at war with each other which allowed the White Boys to get a toehold in the drug game.

"He might work?" Mays pursed her lips and nodded as she read Rabbit's violent history. Whoever ran their drugs would need to be violent because the other gangs would want in.

"Or him," Davis said as watched the next van pull up and unload. One eyed Dino stepped out and looked around his new surroundings. He stretched his legs and rolled his neck once the restraints were removed. It was a long ride and he was eager to get on the fuck shit.

"Ultimately, they're all going to get a way in. I don't mind as long as I get mine," Mays mentioned. She remembered the chaos that came when one group controls too much of the market. The last time that happened it left several dead on the rec yard. They ran the last warden crazy but she had other plans.

"Yes ma'am," her deputy agreed since she was on that same page in a different book. There was a ton of money to be made and she wanted to make it. That's precisely why she made some last minute new hires in the kitchen. She dubbed her new crew, PBTP, because the big, country, young girls were here to sell pussy by the pound.

"Dino Williams. Leader of the notorious Bandos!" Sergeant Pike greeted with a curious enthusiasm. By all accounts the man was a monster but looked more like a male model from up close.

"That's me," he offered along with a perfectly white smile. He had been an ugly duckling as a teen and the girls didn't dig him. That's how he stumbled across some boy pussy in juvenile. He would never admit actually committing a few petty crimes just to lay up in some booty. The murder charge that got him a life sentence was accidental but happened in the course of a rape and those carry life sentences too.

"Plan on raping anyone soon?" She asked offhandedly since his record said he was definitely going to rape someone soon. Not that she cared since she only dealt with gangs.

"Prolly. Unless they giving it up," Dino shrugged nonchalantly. She had his record open so there was no need to lie about it. He noticed her large breast and wide hips even while sitting but they were wasted on him. All he wanted was a pretty little white boy. Or black boy, light skin or dark. Or another Mexican like he had a couple years back. With his black hair, brown skin and...

"Um, excuse me!" Pike interjected and brought him back to the here and now of the present.

"Shit, my bad," Dino laughed and shifted the large erection in his pants that the memories produced.

"Well I see you have another parole date coming soon. Why don't you calm down a little? Maybe you'll make it," she suggested but his face took on a sourpuss look as she spoke.

"Them folks ain't never finna let me go. That's why I do what I do. Especially to white boys," he explained which explained a lot. Most prisoners had no hope and human beings need hope. What's left once all hope is lost?

"Perhaps if you control yourself and control the Bandos..." Pike was saying but his head was already moving from side to side before she reached the end of the statement. She didn't even get to make her made up threat like she had done the others.

"Ain't no controlling the Bandos. We take what we want!" One eyed Dino laughed and stood. He laughed a little harder when her eyes shot down to what was left of the erection.

"Next!" Sergeant Pike barked as he left the room. His laughter stung a bit but he really just wanted a man who looked like a woman.

"Abdul, you up," the officer said to the next man seated outside her office. The man heard him just fine but that wasn't his name so he kept right on reading from a small Arabic Qur'an. The officer figured correctly that he wasn't going to answer to his name being butchered and corrected himself. "Abdus-Salaam."

"Yes," he said and stood. He didn't like directions being pointed at him like a trained seal but let it go since he was tired from the journey.

"Sa'id Abdus-Salaam. As salaamu alaykum!" Pike greeted and raised her fist into a black power salute. The uninformed often mix the two opposites even if they mean well. Orthodox Islam has nothing to do with black power or any other race.

"I'm not in a gang!" Sa'id said firmly and sighed. He had to repeat this from camp to camp to no avail.

"But you are the leader of the Muslims. Hayes, Macon

State, Hancock, here I bet?" Stated like a fact but asked like a question.

"Look lady. I just got off a van. I don't know who the Imam will be," he said truthfully. An other truth was he hoped it wasn't him since it was a lot of work. Plus he had a court date coming and didn't have time for much more.

"Oh, we choose you! The Warden and I think you would be best!" She offered like the position was hers to offer. What they did notice was less blood on Muslim blades whenever he was at the helm. He had mashed the button enough to let it be the known not to fuck with the Muslims unless you want to take a helicopter ride, but none of nonsense that went on at other places.

"Yeah, no it doesn't work like that. Once everyone is here, we'll pick our prayer leader. I'm sure you'll hear about it," he said as he stood and walked out of her office.

"Ok den! Don't make me put a rag on my head!" She laughed to herself once she was by herself. His grey beard, New York accent and tinge of cockiness gave her a slight tingle. It was just Monday and vans would be coming all week.

"Ok den!" Lil-Zay cheered when he and Trouble were assigned to the same dorm. They were assigned different cells since both were going on the top bunk. Bottom bunks were reserved for vets or elderly.

"That's good," Trouble remarked absentmindedly since his mind was elsewhere. Mainly on his woman and child since he would see and touch them both for the first time in months in just a few days. He arrived at his new cell and switched to the moment. A bald, stocky inmate was already inside unpacking his numerous belongings. He has so much shit it looked like they stopped by Walmart on the way.

"What's up Jone!" The man greeted as he came into their new home for however long. A quick once over was all he needed to read Trouble before he spoke.

"Ok den, from that city!" Trouble acknowledged when he heard the unmistakable Atl slang. "They call me Trouble."

"Trouble from the west side? Be with Ridell, Nard 'ndem?" He asked and answered the confused look on his face. "They call me Stack. Off Cascade."

"Oh shit I heard about you!" Trouble recalled. He still wondered how the chain gang legend heard of him since he had been locked up before Trouble was born.

"Cuz I keep my ear to the streets!" Stack laughed and left him to wonder how. Trouble would find out soon enough since they were sharing the same eight by ten foot space.

"What you is?" Lil-Zay's new bunkmate asked and took a defensive stance the second he walked in the cell.

"Rider my nigga!" He proudly proclaimed and ran through a volley of gang signs.

"AUG Roller!" The other inmate from the Augusta Georgia Rollers announced and swung. Just being in the same room as a Rider was enough to fight about.

The boxing ring and MMA octagon have nothing on fighting in an eight by ten cell. The already tight space is even further reduced by a bunk bed, writing desk, locker boxes and a toilet. In other words you better have some hands. If not you might get you head banged against a bunk bed, writing desk, locker boxes and a toilet.

"Man I bet that's my lil homie," Trouble said and shook his head. He joined the others and went to investigate. Both Riders and Rollers converged at the cell to see what was happening. The Rollers wanted to jump in but the Riders would have jumped too. Luckily a vet was on hand to settle the matter.

"That's a one on one. Let 'em hit! Anyone wanna jump y'all can line up outside my door," Stack offered. Then scanned all faces to see who didn't like it. Come to find out, they liked it a lot more than losing teeth so no one budged.

"Twelve!" An inmate announced as two officers rushed into the dorm. They came to investigate before calling a code. Had just rookie officers been present it would have been called in for sure.

"They shooting a one?" The veteran officer asked as the rookie pulled her walkie talkie. He held her off to diffuse it on his own. Its a lot less paperwork that way.

"Roommate shit," someone explained which explained a lot. Shit, family members can't always get along in the same space so how they expect total strangers to is one of many chain gang mysteries.

"Well, that's enough! Break it up!" The veteran officer decided and shook his can of mace just in case the combatants disagreed. Neither did since they were beating the shit out of each other and no one was getting nowhere.

"You good?" The Roller asked Zay as they stepped back.

"Shit you good?" Zay shot back since he had no reverse and didn't know his to back down. Both would fight to the death before backing down. The world is in trouble when black men decide to fight for air, women and children with that same ferocity.

"Yeah y'all good!" A familiar voice insisted and pulled his Roller away. He looked up and saw his cousin for the first time in months.

"Oh shit! Rallo?" Trouble laughed and stepped forward. He had heard he had gotten locked up in the suburbs but had no details. Rallo tensed for combat since he knew why he was here. The look on Trouble's face said he didn't since Malaysia hadn't figured out how to tell him yet.

"Sup cuz," Rallo greeted cautiously. "You talk to Lay-lay 'ndem?"

"Err day. Err body good," he said but the unspoken said he didn't know he robbed their spot.

"Ok den," Rallo nodded. The tensions between the factions died down as their followers watched their leaders talk casually. That may have been good for the gangs but the civilians were in trouble when the gangs aren't beefing. That meant they could turn their attentions towards them. It wasn't unheard of for a civilian to start a lie that would start a war just so the gangs would be too busy to prey on them. Just another peril of life in the chain gang.

Chapter Three

"*A*s salaamu alaykum!" A Muslim inmate greeted when he saw Sa'id walk into the dorm. That wasn't enough so he turned and loudly announced, "Sa'id here!"

"Wa alaykum as salaam," Sa'id greeted and stifled a sigh as several Muslims came out of their cells to either greet or meet him.

He knew from experience that too many Muslims in the dorm can be either good thing or a bad thing. It was usually somewhere in the middle for various reasons. The civilians usually loved a large Muslim presence since it tended to cut down the bullshit. Ironic, since there was generally four of five times as many Christians in every dorm but they refuse to unite and stand up. If, or when they did they would run the chain gang.

The brothers came down to greet the brother and help him tote his property to his cell. Quite a few knew him from other facilities, others heard of him. That's why some were happy to share a dorm with him while others were not. The no nonsense Muslim expected the Muslims to behave like Muslims. That was fine for most but some had habits contrary to Islam.

"So you finna be the Imam?" Mustapha asked hopefully while Shareef hoped in the other direction. Sa'id was known for kicking people like him out of communities. It of course would be easier to comply to what he claimed he was but the devil convinced him otherwise. One thing about the devil, he's consistent.

"Hope not," Sa'id said and shook his head since he knew it wasn't up to him. He knew nothing really is, since everything has already been written.

"I heard Jahil here!" Mustapha announced. He was another well know Imam throughout the system. The two had heard of each other but never did time together.

"In sha Allah," Sa'id said verbally while mentally acquiescing the position to him. That way he could focus in his upcoming court date as well as not be held responsible for everything some of the so-called Muslims were sure to do. The real Muslims were sure to get caught up in it when they did. The Muslims weren't the only ones greeting one of their own.

"Ooh chile, Dino here!" A sissy fawned and cheered as yet another chain gang legend entered the dorm. Some were known for their fight game, others for their hustle or ability to pull female employees. Some like Stack were known for all of the above but One eyed Dino was known for the fuck-shit.

From camp to camp he had been raping and pillaging like a band of Vikings through an English country side. Other like- minds joined him since they couldn't beat him and formed the Bandos. Taking booty was better than having the booty taken but some dudes ended up liking it and became girls. Just like these three Dino had raped into submission through the decades.

"Uh-oh! Not Cupcake and Honey Bun!" He cheered. For some reason the chain gang sissies take on sugary snacks for names. Odd since cupcakes don't taste like shit. Nor is eating a honey-bun the same as eating ass.

"Mmhm daddy! Gingerbread, Short Cake and Apple Pie here too!" Honey Bun informed. Sergeant Pike made sure to spread the Bandos and their make believe broads out evenly just like any other gang. It was like shuffling the deck and dealing the cards face up so no one could run a Boston.

"Ok then," he nodded and sat his stuff down in the middle of the floor. The sissies quickly scooped it up and carried them to his new cell where his new bunk-mate was putting away his stuff.

"Sup bruh! I'm JJ. A-town Roller!" JJ greeted. He made sure to state his affiliation despite snitching on Rallo. That rooster hadn't come home to roost just yet so he was a Roller for the time being.

"Dino," Dino greeted and let the eyepatch explain the rest. There was no shocked look of name recognition which could only mean one thing. "You 'musta just got locked up?"

"Hell yeah. Messing around out there in Cobb County. Them crackers gave me a dub!" He lied since the truth was he was a snitch. He doubled his time to twenty years to seem tough.

"Yeah, gotta keep your dirt in the hood," Dino said. He heard the man say he was gang related but knew enough to know that didn't always matter so he tried him up. The shared toilet is next to the door so it's customary to face the door and turn your back to the bunkmate when taking a leak. Not Dino though he faced the interior of the room and whipped out.

"Oh my bad!" JJ said and spun around.

Dino hummed. He caught the quick glance at the dick before he turned. That's how it starts, and that's his shit started. The child molester was also dumped in the same dorm but that was done on purpose. Pike had been 'touched' as a girl too and got get back when and where she could.

"You straight?" Honey blBun squealed as they returned. Cupcake went to make up the bed while the other folded Dino's clothes and placed them in the locker box.

"Shit y'all straight? Ain't nobody brang nothing down here?" Dino answered with a question of his own.

"You gots to know we did!" Cupcake said all sassy like sissies do. They think they're mimicking women but most women aren't as feminine. Not only, after decades of having to support themselves and their children like men. Only because some men are fuck men in one or two senses. Fuck men like these men who literally fuck men. Or fuck men who refuse to take care of their kids.

To be fair, some women are fuck men too if they refuse to let a man take care of their children just because they don't want them. Lots of good father's are shut out of their kids lives for this reason.

"Ta-dah!" Honey Bun announced like a magic trick as he produced a thick joint. Then came out with some rolled up cigarettes.

"She brought half a can of tobacco and I got eight ounces!" Cupcake explained.

"Y'all packed them suitcases full!" Dino cheered while poor JJ was so confused.

"You made them like that daddy!" Honey Bun giggled coyly. A far cry from the cries when Dino raped him way back when.

"I ain't get no suitcase tho?" JJ asked and looked between them all. He sure would have brought some weed or tobacco too if he had.

"Yeah you do. I'll show it to you later," Dino offered and cracked the sissies up. "You can smoke with us if you? Just pay when you get straight."

"Uh-oh!" Cupcake laughed. This was the very definition of writing a check that your ass can't cash. Or can, since that's where he would collect from.

"Who the fuck is that?" Dino demanded when a smiling face appeared in the window.

"Chile that's Merle, my bunk-mate," Honey Bun replied shaking his head. "He like to mess with kids!"

"Sho nuff?" Dino asked enthusiastically. There was no one he liked raping more than men who messed with kids.

They could report him all they liked because the staff didn't care. Why should anyone care about someone getting what they deserved.

"Hail Rabbit!" A white boy who happened to be a White Boy proclaimed and thrust a Nazi like salute in the air when he saw his god walk through the door. The other White Boys in the dorm all stopped what they were doing to get a glimpse of the man the followed and fought for.

"How many of us are here?" Rabbit asked as he marched to his cell. He had another question before he reached, "They ain't put me with a nigga did they?"

"Cell eighteen?" The White Boy said and strained to recall who was in that room. "No. He's white! A civilian."

"No such thing," Rabbit laughed since he had the power of persuasion for Caucasians. He managed to smuggle in a shit load of meth in a baby powder bottle. The guards made sure to make sure nothing was hidden in the powder but didn't think to check what the powder actually was. Besides, they had a white supremist in the white house for four years so anything was possible.

"Hey guys! I'm Herbert," Rabbit's nerdy new bunkmate greeted as the men entered the cell. He extended his hand for shaking but Rabbit ignored it.

"A fucking chester?" Rabbit surmised in an instant. The pasty, pudgy man definitely wasn't in here for thugging so it had to be for messing with children.

"No, um Herbert," he repeated and wagged the outstretched hand.

"No, your new name is Chester the Molester!" One of the White Boys demanded and knocked the hand away. Rabbit smiled that lopsided smile and decided he liked the aggressive dude.

"What they call you?" He asked as he scanned the man's tattoos for a clue.

"Ghost!" He said at the same time Rabbit made out the word on his forehead. Small ghost designs filled in the elaborate artwork that adorned every visible surface of his skin. He may have hated black people but was damn near black himself with all that ink.

"That's Lieutenant Ghost from now on! I need a count and location by Lock down. Everyone on the yard, first yard call," Rabbit dictated. Ghost was a lieutenant but he was the president.

"There was just a misunderstanding, I don't know how those pictures got on my computer! I never touched any..." Chester was explaining to people who weren't listening. It didn't matter because Rabbit would put him to use too. White power needs man power and he would need to be put to work whether he liked it or not.

"Anyways, I don't know about this Connor dude upstairs. Uppity fucking white boy from Buckhead," the other White Boy called Inferno announced.

The rich kid caught a couple years for forging his daddy the doctor's name on prescriptions. A few of those pills got into the hands of a rich girl who took a few too many and died. Pretty much the same as thing Rabbit earned a life sentence for. Except, Connor's rich parents were able to outbid the girls parents for justice and he ended up with a ten year sentence, with only two to serve. He would quietly be paroled in months and back doing the same shit. Because it's not called white privilege for nothing.

"Like I said, no such thing!" Rabbit reiterated. There was always some he couldn't recruit but they always wished they did. By the time they got the point the offer was off the table and they were left to the wolves.

The chain gang is full of wolves.

Chapter Four
_____

"Yard call!" The dorm officer called. Most of the dorm moved since most were affiliated and had orders to meet up at first yard call. It was time to take stock and get organized.

The staff knew the more energy the men and boys exerted on the yard was less energy to exert on each other. Pretty much the same principal mothers had been using on toddlers for centuries. Tire their little asses out and put them down for a good night's sleep. A lot of these grown men were a lot like toddlers. Big, muscular, dangerous toddlers, always getting into shit.

"You going out?" Trouble asked when he saw Stack pulling on yet another a pair of tennis shoes.

He had one pair to walk around in, one pair to work out in as well as a pair of new Jordan's wrapped in plastic for visitation. Trouble took notice but didn't ask any questions. That was a good sign for the vet who was sizing him up as well. The streets spoke highly of the youngin but the chain gang exposes things in some people they didn't know was in there themselves.

"Hell yeah. Hit this bar, 'politic a lil," he said and turned to leave the cell.

Trouble waited on Lil-Zay and lined up to be signed out. Everything was being done by the book since the veteran officers were still training the new recruits. Once that was done they would introduce them to the shortcuts that the chain gang really operates on. They performed the counts by the book but later wouldn't count at all. No one was going anywhere anyway so it always added up.

The new jack inmates were also getting trained by the vets. Each group hit the yard and spread out to claim there individual area. No signs were needed but the boundaries were written in stone once they were established.

The Rollers and Riders each claimed a basketball court and the bleacher in front of it. The White Boys claimed one and left the last one for the civilians. The Mexicans took control of the soccer field while the Muslims claimed a bleacher under an awning.

One eyed Dino claimed the furthest bleacher for the Bandos since they preferred a little privacy. Those who knew him would have reserved it for him anyway because Dino didn't care where he got down with the get down. His philosophy was don't look if you don't want to see.

The pull-up bars were universal and everyone could use them. There were usually representatives from every faction who liked to work out. Mutual respect for the workout was usually enough to keep order.

"Sup Jone!" Stack heard behind him and turned to see

who was using his trademark word. It could only be a friend since foes didn't speak like that.

"Sup Jone!" He shot back when he saw a face he hadn't seen in over a decade. He and Sa'id were bunkmates back when Sa'id first hit the system. He taught him the ropes and rules he still lived by. The two men dapped like dudes do and kicked it.

"Where you been since we left that spot?" Sa'id asked. He watched the flow of kufis going to the Muslim territory and would head over once they caught up.

"Everywhere!" Stack said and named the whirlwind of camps he had been to. Some for a second time since they hadn't paroled him yet. The state of Georgia would rather stack men three high than let them go home.

"Me too," Sa'id said and rattled off a smaller list of facilities.

"I see you got that book shit popping Jone!" Stack congratulated where lots of dudes just hated. Sa'id showed him the couple books he had written and Stack urged him to mash the gas with it. Now he had sold hundreds of thousands of books from prison and had a movie in the making.

"A lil something," he said humbly since to Allah went the credit. "Going back to court soon tho. In sha Allah, I'm about to give this time back!"

"In sha Allah," Stack repeated since he too knew everything is subject to God's will. We can't even will unless Allah wills. "We'll catch up!"

"Fa sho," Sa'id agreed and dapped him up once more. Stack hit the bar while Sa'id followed the trail of kufis to where the Muslims posted up. "As salaamu alaykum ikhwan!"

"Wa alaykum as salaam!" The men greeted in return. Some amped up the blessing with a, "Ramatullahi wa barakatuhu."

"We finally meet!" Jahil greeted and extended his hand to be shook. He gave him a quick once over as they greeted each other. Rumor had it that the brother made a nice piece of change in the book world but he certainly wasn't wearing it. He wore regular sneakers off the prison catalog and his shorts came from the commissary. "I hear good things about you!"

"Masha Allah!" Sa'id said as they shook. He had heard plenty about him as well but it wasn't all good. He gave him a quick once over as well and registered the new Jordan's, free world shorts and gold chain and ring.

The fancy clothes and shoes weren't a crime in themselves even if crimes paid for them. The gold on his hands, on the other hand were forbidden for Muslim men. In Islam adornments like gold and silk are reserved for the women. His clean shaven face was also forbidden for a variety of reasons. Sa'id chose to ignore all of it for his own personal agenda.

"So, which one of y'all finna be Imam?" One brother cut straight to the chase and asked. He had heard of both but hadn't met either and had no opinion either way.

"I guess we can have a vote," Jahil offered and made Sa'id flinch at the irregularity. There was no voting on a prayer leader since the criteria had been set over fourteen hundred years before. The person with the most knowledge of the Qur'an obviously should lead the prayer.

"No voting akhi, remember?" Sa'id said like a reminder but had the suspicion he didn't know. He did memorize quite a bit of Qur'an but kept it to himself. Instead of stepping up as he should he bowed out and let him have it. He knew it was the wrong decision just as surely as he knew it would come back to bite him. Still he said, "I'm getting ready to go back to court, so you can lead the prayer."

"Ok then!" Jahil cheered and cheesed happily. Far more happily than any person should, given the gravity of the responsibility he'd undertaken. Not just in the sight of Allah, but the life or death daily decisions of the chain gang. "You can assist me!"

"In sha Allah," Sa'id sighed. Sixteen years into his illegal conviction, he just wanted to go home.

Some people had issues with him writing those street books despite the positive messages. Still, there's a big difference between writing about a dope boy than actually being a dope boy.

"Hail Rabbit!" Each of the White Boys greeted as they joined the group on the bleachers.

All tallied, they totaled more than any of the other groups except the Mexicans. That's because a good number weren't even actually from Mexico. Whoever spoke Spanish was counted among them, no matter where they hailed from. There were quite a few black faces from Panama, Honduras, Cuba and Guatemala.

"Looks like the gangs all here!" Ghost announced once members from every dorm were present. He took a quick count and names so they could know who was who. Now it was time for their leader to speak.

Rabbit walked to the front of the bleachers but didn't speak. Ghost opened his mouth to shut up the chatter among the men but Rabbit waved him off. His presence alone made his point and the banter died down.

"White power is the only power," he offered plainly as if it were a matter of fact and not an opinion.

"White power!" The men roared back and turned heads. Some black civilians heard them as they walked by but wasn't anything they could do about. The gangs might not have liked it had they heard it but they were outnumbered.

"We're in a new facility that's wide open. We will get a toehold and control the methamphetamine trade," he stated as if that too was a matter of fact. He was off to a good start since he was able to smuggle in a few ounces of the hot commodity.

As he spoke Ghost handed a few prepackaged sacks of the drug to the head of each dorm. All eyes lit up since ninety nine percent of the gang were addicts. Rabbit had sworn off the stuff that led to the death of his mother that earned him a life sentence.

"Fifty/fifty split," Ghost explained to each man he handed the drugs to. They could sell it, snort it, shoot or stick it up their assess as long as Rabbit got what he was supposed to get.

"Once the pipeline is wide open we will..." Rabbit was saying while also keeping watchful eyes around the yard. He saw the one eye of One Eyed Dino and stopped dead in his tracks. He felt a sharp phantom pain in his anus when he saw the man who raped him decades ago. Dino saw him too.

"What daddy?" Honey Bun asked when their war daddy's face turned to stone. He too had been scanning the yard like a periscope with his one eye when he spotted the person who took his other eye. He too felt a stabbing phantom pain in the eye that was no longer there.

"Huh? Nothing. Just saw an old friend," Dino remarked and he and Rabbit locked the three eyes between them. Neither spoke but both made an unspoken vow to kill the other. Real beef doesn't die until someone is dead.

"This the fuck nigga I was telling you about," Rallo mumbled to Mac Town when he spotted JJ looking around. JJ spotted the crew of Rollers and began to come over.

"Shit, we woulda kilt that nigga in county!" Mac Town grunted. He was the leader of the Macon faction of Rollers so he was promoted to be Rallo's right hand man.

"Nigga caught PC, couldn't get to him," Rallo remarked out the side of his mouth as JJ arrived.

"Sup shawty, here!" JJ greeted and paid homage with a thick stick of weed. Joints of reefer are usually the size of a mosquito leg but this one was as fat as the free world.

"Fuck you get weed from?" Rallo needed to know. The Cobb County Jail was dry as a desert and he hadn't smoked in months.

"My bunkmate Dino! He's cool as fuck! Gave me a fat sack to smoke on and I can pay him later," JJ said naively. He had that exact same look in his eyes as a deer in some headlights. Right before getting ran the fuck over.

"One eyed Dino? Bruh..." Mac asked incredibly. He

had been in juvie with the monster when he killed the boy, then fucked him.

"Cool, get as much as you can!" Rallo cut in and cut Mac Town off before he could warn him.

"Ok, I'll be back!" JJ said and happily traipsed over to Dino and his crew.

"Say bruh, Dino gonna rape that boy if he don't pay," Mac warned.

"Mmhm. And we gonna sell the nigga to him," Rallo laughed and took a big pull off the weed. He was learning a real lesson in power, never get your hands dirty.

"What you see?" Warden Mays asked as she and her deputy watched the yard from above. It was a test so she listened carefully for her answer.

"Well..." She sighed and paused to compose her thoughts. She has seen plenty and now had to articulate it, while holding some back to keep her own avenue open. "The White Boys got some dope. Not sure if its a little or a lot, but something."

"Probably suitcased it in like the sissies," Mays surmised since a steady cloud of smoke hovered above Dino and company since they came out. They definitely had there own because they were smoking too much to have paid chain gang prices.

"Mexicans are deep. They can handle distribution," Davis offered.

"They are, they can," she agreed and looked over to the black gangs. She could see the admiration Trouble garnered from his crew. The other leaders lead from fear, this was love.

"He does have a conspiracy charge," Davis added when she saw where she was looking. She hoped the warden would pick a team so she could pick one for herself.

"You know what?" Mays asked hypothetically then answered since the woman couldn't read her mind. "We're going to eat off all of them! They're all going to find a way in so why pick one? They're all going to pay!"

"Smart!" Davis cheered because it was. It cancelled her plans of using one of the gangs or groups but she still had other irons in the fire. Prisons are gold mines and she was a gold digger.

Chapter Five

"You not going to chow?" Trouble asked a couple hours after they returned from the yard.

"Shawty I ain't been to the chow hall in twenty years!" Stack laughed. Trouble couldn't laugh since he had only been alive that long.

"I better fill me out a commissary order so I can get my locker box straight too," he said since Malaysia kept a nice piece of money on his books. He didn't know it was the last of it since she hadn't told him about the theft yet. She planned to make the drive down and tell him face to face this weekend. Perhaps holding his son for the first time would take some of the sting out of it.

"Hell yeah.If you need something tho..." Stack extended the open offer since he knew the youngin was good for it.

"Appreciate it," he said graciously even though he would never take him up on it. He had been hungry before but never asked anyone for anything. Instead, he went out and got his.

Trouble and Rallo nodded but didn't speak since each was with their respective gang. Them living in peace was proof the rest could as well. Even though the young boys were itching to get into something. If no drugs came in to soothe their nerves it was going to be a problem. Several problems.

"Two more seconds and I woulda had that nigga," Lil-Zay said when he and the Roller he fought saw each other.

"I know it!" Trouble agreed whether it was true or not. They both had their hands full and it could have went either way. Both stopped to look at the menu posted on the wall.

"Ok den, chicken and dressing! My granny be fixing that!" Zay cheered of the familiar food. They walked to the chow hall with visions of white fluffy rice and big chunks of chicken laced throughout. It said green beans, sweet potatoes and rolls as well so they were all for it.

Neither took into account that since it was three thirty in the afternoon, it would make for a long night with no food in their locker. Both had plenty in the county but weren't allowed to take any of it down the road. They blessed the Riders in the dorm with it before they left.

"Shit smell good!" Trouble announced as they entered the chow hall and got in line.

"Rollers in 'dih bih!" A young banger proclaimed as he led two more to the front of the line.

"Don't skip the line young blood," a vet at the front of the line politely stated. The kids looked him up and down, taking in his age, thick glasses and soft speech. It's a mystery why that added up to weakness to them but it did. They missed the thick forearms and danger in the irises though.

"Nigga fu..." The kid was saying just before getting knocked out. His partners who had his back backed away with their hands up. Kept backing up until they reached the back of the line.

"There's a lesson in that," Trouble quipped.

"A couple," Lil-Zay added since he caught more than one. First, respect your elders. Dude had been away from his family for thirty years and had zero tolerance for disrespect. Second not to judge a book because the outside may not match the inside.

They both learned the lesson that the food sounds a lot better on the menu than it looks on the trays. Partly because part of breakfast was still on the trays. They were still at the county jail when grits were served that morning but some remained on the tray until dinner.

They both also realized that chicken part of the chicken was the parts people don't usually eat. Gristle, skin and tendons were boiled tasteless and added to under cooked rice. The yams tasted just like the can they came out of and the green beans looked like they had been chewed already.

"The rolls good!" Trouble, the eternal optimist said as he bit into one. Both plucked their rolls off the tray and took the trays to the tray window. Neither made it.

"Y'all not eating that?" A man asked before they could slide them into the window to be half cleaned for breakfast.

"Naw dad. Here," Zay said solemnly and handed his over. So did Trouble and he sat down in front of the pile of trays he collected with scraps of food. He did what he had to do to go to bed with a full stomach. An empty

41

stomach will wake a man from his sleep quicker than a full bladder.

~

"How was yo dinner?" Stack laughed when Trouble returned to their cell.

"You 'coulda warned a nigga!" He laughed along with him.

"Some lessons gotta be learned the hard way," the vet explained. "I hooked us up a pocket."

"Appreciate it unc," he said genuinely. He was prepared to bite the bullet and go to bed hungry if he had to. What he would not do was ask. Stack was still whipping up the chain gang delicacy while Trouble went to fill out a commissary request on the kiosk. Lil-Zay met him over there to do the same.

"Where we at, the airport or some shit!'" Zay fussed when he saw the overpriced items for sale.

"Fifty cent for a ramen damn noodle. Them shits twelve for a dollar at the store!" Trouble said, shaking his head. Everything was five to ten times more expensive than it would be on the street. Probably why they don't parole people out since they're making so much money off of them.

"Shit, it's either that or chicken guts and gristle!" Lil-Zay said and completed his order.

"Say shawty. If y'all need a lil something until they run 'sto just holla. I got the two for ones," another vet offered since he transferred in with several net bags full of food. The prison was bad enough with their high prices but the usury of the store man was worse. Zay opened his mouth to accept the offer but his partner got off first.

"Bruh, I'm mad about paying the fiddy cent for a soup. The fuck I look paying a dollar?" Trouble needed to know. He even waited for an answer but the vet didn't have one. Two for ones are for suckers or addicts. These two were neither. The inmate shrugged it off and found a couple of suckers to pay his price.

"Grab ya bowl Jone. I ain't the butler," Stack barked when Trouble returned. "Got some extra for ya 'potna."

"Wait!" Trouble shouted urgently when Stack attempted to drop a wire plugged into the socket into the bucket of water. He shoved him as hard as he could before he could be electrocuted.

"Fuck you doing Jone?" Stack wondered as he bounced off the wall.

"Saving your life shawty! You almost put a live current in water!" He replied. His face twisted in confusion when Stack cracked up. The explanation would have to wait a few minutes as he got a hearty laugh out.

"Bruh this how we boil water and cook our food!" He explained and demonstrated. He put the wires back in the water and sure enough it came to a rolling boil.

"Bruh let me find out you chef in this bitch!" Trouble laughed when he inhaled what can be done with those high ass commissary items. The three ate and filled uncle Stack in on what was happening around the hood. He knew or knew of everyone out there.

"You Jenel son ain't you?" Stack figured from the names associated with Trouble.

"Please tell me you ain't my daddy!" Trouble laughed when he named his mama's name.

"Naw, but I know yo daddy. You looks just like him!" He laughed now that he knew why the kid looked so familiar.

"Phones on yet?" Trouble asked to kill two birds with the same stone. One he really did need to hear his woman's voice and his son's coos. Second, he wasn't ready to hear about the man he never met.

"Naw, but handle yo biz. I'm finna hop in the shower," Stack said and handed him a cell phone. Trouble blinked at it in his hand like he wasn't sure what it was. He opened his mouth to ask how, then closed it back.

"Appreciate it," he said and quickly dialed one of the few numbers he had committed to memory.

"Hello!" Malaysia snapped into the phone at the strange number.

"Can I speak to Malaysia?" He said in a made up voice.

"Who is dis!" She remanded instead of asking since the few who had her number should definitely know her voice.

"Pedro, from da club," Trouble managed without laughing because he could just picture her face twisted up on the other side of the call.

"You a lie and yo mami is a bitch!" She snapped and clicked off. Trouble cracked up and called back but was promptly sent to voice mail.

"Shit!" He fussed when he realized on the fourth try that she wasn't picking up. He stopped trying to call and sent a text message instead. The phone buzzed two seconds later from her number.

"Trouble!" Malaysia shouted so loudly he had to pull

the phone from his ear. 'You play too much! I miss you! I love you! How you calling me?"

"Uh," he paused to put the answers in order. "My bad. I miss you too shawty. Love you. Shit my potna got a cell phone in this bitch!"

"You down the road?" She asked since phones are off in the county jail when they ship out.

"Hell yeah. D-Block," he said. "Oh! Guess who here?"

"Boy we from he hood! It could be any damn body!" She laughed and put her hand on her hip just like he pictured in his head.

"True. Yo damn cousin! They got me and Rallo in the same damn dorm. I guess we supposed to keep our cliques in line. They saying I can be out this bitch early if we do," he said and got silence in reply.

Malaysia wanted to explain to him about the burglary their bitch ass cousin committed but not at the expense of him coming home. She would tell him about the money when she came to see him but decided to leave that part out.

"Oh Ok. So, you know we coming down this weekend!" She gushed. It would take almost all of what she had left but she needed to see him just as bad as he needed to see her. A soulmate is a lot like oxygen in some ways. Both give you life.

"Hell yeah! Finally get to touch my woman and hold my son!" He cheered all for it. They caught up for the next few minutes until Stack returned.

"You straight shawty?" He asked as he returned.

"Yes sir, 'preciate it," Trouble said and handed the phone back. It's customary to surrender the room when the bunkmate returns from the shower so he grabbed his hygiene items and headed out.

Except for Dino and JJ since Dino told him he was good when he came from his shower. JJ turned his back while the man applied lotion to his skin and powdered his balls. He had no idea One eyed Dino was trying him up again.

That was day one in the chain gang.

Chapter Six

*L*alonda was already awake when the alarm began it's irritating buzz. It only served to irritate the irate woman even more. Life was far from ideal but she was able to place a finger on was particularly irking her this morning. Her rotation at work began today and the inmates began arriving yesterday. It was showtime and she wasn't sure if she was ready.

"Turn that shit off!" Marcus moaned when the buzz interrupted his slumber.

"Yeah cuz it's not like you finna get up and go to work," she snarled down at him. She looked him up and down in disgust until she saw the morning wood poking through the hole in his boxer shorts. In better days she would wake up with it pressed against her backside. She would grind her ass on it until Marcus awoke. Then he would lift her leg and slide into her. He would nibble on the back of her neck while delivering solid back shots until they both shuddered from a mutual orgasm.

"What you doing?" Marcus fussed when Lalonda scooted her backside against the dick. A good nut would calm her nerves for work.

"Tryna get laid," she purred and reached back and gripped the wood. He didn't lift her leg like the days gone by but she was perfectly capable of lifting her own leg. She also did the honors and worked him inside of her. She was slippery wet from anticipation and starvation since they hadn't had sex in a while.

"Shit!" Marcus grunted when her tight, hot box engulfed him. Certainly a big difference from Sheryl's big box. He took over and lifted that leg a little higher so he could dig his wife out properly. And dig her out he did. The splashes and smacks of her juice box and skin slapping filled the room.

"Oooh, you finna make me nut!" Lalonda whined and did just that. With not a split second to spare.

"Fuck!" Marcus groaned and went stiff as he skeeted in his wife. "Damn Sheryl, you got some good ass pussy!"

"Mmhm," she said and rolled off the bed. She went into the bathroom to pee and shower so she could go to work to support a man who just called her by the next bitch's name.

Marcus was sound asleep by the time she showered and dressed for work. That meant she had to admire herself in her uniform so she took a moment in front of the full length mirror to do just that. She couldn't help but compare her apple shaped ass to the Sponge Bob, square pants ass of the woman her husband just called her.

"Tuh!" She decided since he was tripping, not her. Her head was lifted high as she stepped out and drove to work.

Lalonda had know idea she had parked in the exact same spot officer Daryl Johnson blew his brains out a few months prior. Not that there were many options since the large lot was filled since both shifts were there at the moment. It would reduce by almost half once night shift was relieved. Almost half, since more staff worked days than nights.

She cocked her head curiously as four large, country girls filed out a mini van. They all wore kitchen steward uniforms which explained their presence. Lalonda wondered how much that position paid and if they had to be in direct contact with the inmates. That was the part that still unnerved her. Little did she know the PBTP would have far more contact with the inmates than she could imagine.

Just like her brother before her, Lalonda was one of the first to arrive in the briefing room. They picked up the same good traits from the same good parenting but just like Chuck, D-Block would test those limits.

"Good morning Williams!" Another bright eyed officer greeted as she was second to arrive. They finished in the same order in training class with Lalonda slightly ahead.

"Good morning Atkins. They here," Lalonda said and heard the apprehension in her own voice. The good nut helped relax her a little but her husband fucked it up by calling her the wrong name.

"I heard!" She said since the two thousand men made a lot of noise. It would be even louder once the facility was full, then overcrowded. Likewise the briefing room filled with banter as it filled with officers.

"Good morning, let's get started!" The lieutenant

greeted as he took the podium with his sergeant at his side. He opened his mouth to speak but the door opened before he could.

"Warden on deck!" The sergeant announced and snapped to attention. The chairs made noises as they were quickly abandoned by the officers coming to attention as well.

"Carry-on!" Warden Mays said once she was satisfied that everyone stood for her. She took over the podium to handle the morning briefing. The vets had been scheduled to accept the inmates but now the rookies were here as well. "The ladies of D-Block were some dangerous bitches! The men, will be even more so. There are locks, locks and more locks followed by gates, razor wire and more gates. Patrol cars with shotguns and forty caliber pistols.

Those are the means to keep the prisoners inside the prison. That is not your job. Your job is not to punish, or add to the punishment. Your number one duty is to clock out at the end of the day just like you clocked in this morning. These men are killers, murderers, rapist, oh and killers! Do your job and let them do their time. We are outnumbered many, many times over. Control is just an illusion, they run this motherfucker! If they go crazy we're in trouble! All we can do is call for help from state patrol..."

'Fuck!' Lalonda thought to herself as she listened to the straightforward facts. They were taught the exact opposite in the brief academy. The trainers taught them to oppress and control. Dominate and demean but the warden was singing a different tune.

Some officers, vets and new jacks took heed, others decided to stick to their training. Lalonda remembered her brothers advice fell somewhere in the middle. The middle course was always best. He husband wasn't shit but she did want to come home to him at the end of the day.

"Well..." The lieutenant said once he got the stage back. That's not quite how he would have said it but it was said. He wouldn't contradict it so he moved on to the next issue. "Rookies, day shift is earned. You'll get a week in with the vets before moving to nights next week."

Night shift was actually the better shift since there was far less contact with inmates. There was usually just the church services to sign out at night and breakfast call in the morning. Once the inmates locked down at night they could just chill. They ducked inspections and didn't have to deal with the administration. Perfect position to be in to do dirt.

Lalonda was assigned to a white veteran officer named Jolly. The irony of his name didn't escape her since he was one cynical motherfucker. He had bounced around the department for nearly two decades but couldn't make rank. That was affirmative action, Jesse Jackson and Al Sharpton's fault. Everyone's but his own.

"I know you people don't like men to hold doors for you," he said over his shoulder as he let the door close behind him. Lalonda wasn't sure if 'her people' meant black or women so she held her tongue for now. They arrived at their assigned dorm and greeted the night shift officers.

"Good morning!" Both outgoing officers greeted their relief and handed over the book.

"We need to do a changeover count before, signing the book!" Jolly explained. It was fine by Lalonda since that's how she was trained. The night shift officers blew their breath in frustration of having to wait a few minutes longer to get home or to their second jobs.

"Who working?" One eyed Dino asked since it mattered. Cool officers made for a cool day. Monkey officers meant ducking and dodging all day, or waiting until next shift to do dirt.

"Oh hell! That's monkey ass Jolly from down south! Prolly got ran off! Oh and some lady," Honey-bun reported. They were vets themselves and waited to see who was working days before firing up the first joint of the day.

"Guess it'll hold til yard call," Dino shrugged. He was at a prison with Jolly before and knew he would overreact to smelling smoke. Honey Bun and Cupcake headed to their own cells since it was count time.

"Count time! By your door! Hands by your side! Nothing in your hands!" Lalonda barked just like she was taught in the academy. Jolly nodded his head approvingly as she went by the book he knew so well.

The book requires one officer to count while the other stood by. Once the first count was down they would trade places for the second count. If numbers added up they announced "clear" and left the dorm. The quicker the better for both inmates and cops.

Lalonda headed up the stairs to count the top row first. It seemed every other cell only had one man standing beside it. She found out why once she reached the first cell. There was the other man standing over the toilet with his dick hanging out. She assumed he was using the toilet and counted him in placed. That was the first real live dick she seen besides her husband in her life. The next cell contained the third dick, then a fourth and...

"Shit!" Lalonda fussed when the fifth dick made her lose count. The dorm erupted in laughter when she had to start over. This time she looked at faces and got through her first official count. She traded with Jolly and he came up with the same number.

"Clear!" Jolly confirmed and cleared the dorm. Dino and the other vets knew he would be in and out all day so they would wait until yard call to smoke.

"Clear Atkins!" Announced by the same book Lalonda was on. Her veteran partner wasn't with it but correctly assumed he would snitch on him if he deviated. He would put up with her for the week until she was moved to nights and he had the joint to himself.

"Good count," he played along since she would he out his hair next week. "Stand by for classification!"

"What's that?" Trouble asked as Stack traded the Nike slides he wore around the dorm for a pair of tennis shoes. Some prisons were so turned up that sneakers or boots had to worn at all times, but it was laid back for now.

Trouble didn't have any slides or tennis shoes yet so the crocs pulled double duty as around the dorm and around the compound. Some inmate's crocs would pull triple and quadruple duty as gym shoes as well church shoes. Trouble was one of many who would buy some tennis shoes from the state vendor first chance he got.

"Where they assign you a job," Stack said. They were staffing the prison details on the fly since it was quickly filling up.

"Shit I ain't tryna work! Just finna chill and read," Trouble announced. He was a dope boy and dope boys don't work.

"Ain't tryna tell you how to do your time," Stack began, then pause before continuing. "You buck detail you get a disciplinary report. Then when its time to come up for parole you get set off cuz you ain't wanna work."

"Shit, which job pay the most?" He shot back, like say no more. He was with whatever it took to get back home as soon as possible.

"Georgia prisons don't pay! Shit they pay you no mind!" Stack laughed. "Find you a job that work for you! A hustle so prison will pay for itself!"

"I see why they call you Stack!" Trouble laughed when he caught on.

"They can call me 'Stacked' now cuz I got my check all the way up! I'm just chilling now so I can parole out and spend some," he sighed.

"Well, players become coaches once they retire. Put me in coach!" He said seriously. He wasn't down for working for free but a hustler will always hustle.

"Say less shawty. See where they put you and I'll put you on game!" The vet told the new jack. The officers weren't the only ones getting trained.

Chapter Seven

"Hello Chaplain Gayle," Warden Mays greeted the new Chaplain. She made sure to speak loud just in case the odd looking older lady couldn't hear well.

"Hello there warden ma'am," she greeted back. Her head bobbled when she spoke as if the plastic looking wig she wore was too heavy. She was short and morbid looking dressed in all black. The black wedges she wore were a size too big but a sale is a sale.

She was selected for being an old lady more for her religiosity. The last chaplain was fucking everything moving so she picked the seventy year old to cut that out. Of course the warden knew first hand since she had her hands on this same desk while the old chaplain dug her out from the back.

"You want me to assign an officer to you?" The warden offered. She would hope the men would respect the woman but one never can tell. Respect is reciprocal, as in it takes some to get some.

"No ma'am, the Lawd will take care of me!" She vowed and clamped her monkey paw hands together. The wrinkled old hands looked like they hand help dig the underground railroad.

"Yes he will," Mays agreed halfheartedly. She had more faith in the almighty dollar than some deity she couldn't see. Even though He was closer to her than her jugular vein. More importantly she really didn't have the manpower to spare.

"I have my special anointed oil that releases the demons from the men! It soothes them so they won't fuck each other in their asses. They'll fuck you know," the old lady declared and made the warden choke on the sip of coffee she had just sipped.

"Excuse me?" Warden Mays chuckled more from amusement than shock. If the men were anything like the women there would definitely be some fucking. That's probably the most cruel part of the punishment of imprisonment. It brings out unusual behavior in some men and women. Precisely why more progressive states allow conjucal visits. They found violence decreased dramatically with some pussy at stake.

"The men, they fuck," Chaplain Jordan nodded. Her eyes went even bigger behind the magnification of her glasses and cracked the warden up even more.

"Well, feel free to anoint as many as you can!" She laughed. She was still laughing when she walked by the line of men seated outside the office waiting to be seen. Some were here to interview for the chaplain's aid, others in need of bibles and other spiritual guidance.

"First man!" Chaplain Jordan called from behind her desk. The first man in line stood and walked in. The smile on her face took a slightly sinister tone when she registered the white man. "What do you need?"

"Just some prayer ma'am. My mom is in the hospital and..." He was saying but didn't reach said.

"Hail Mary," the woman announced and crossed the air. She wasn't even Catholic but was prejudice as fuck and wanted the white man out of her office as quickly as possible. The woman had lived in the south long enough to see many, many, too many injustices. The disproportionate rate of black incarceration irked her whole soul. This office was her only weapon so she wielded it with impunity. The only people in lower esteem than whites were the homosexuals. She hated homos of any race but held a degree more hatred for the black ones. She knew the lack of black fathers directly attributed to the black men behind bars.

"Thank you ma'am, but..."

"Next!" She called over his shoulder, dismissing him. He looked confused but she looked straight through him until he got the hint and walked out.

The next few men were there to interview for the chapel aid position. The counselors had made the short list of candidates but it was up to her to pick two. She had already been through their files and made her choices. Everyone would still get an interview to seem fair.

"Good morning ma'am," Stack greeted as he came into the office. He stood until a seat was offered like a gentlemen should.

"Good morning dear. Have a seat," she said with her head bobbling. "Why they call you Stack?"

"Cuz I used to stack dollars," he admitted with a shrug. If she knew his chain gang nickname he was pretty sure she knew the answers to the rest of her questions. She did, but asked them anyway.

"Can you fight? Cuz sometimes I gotta run some of these men off," she explained.

"I can fight but you need to call the cops to remove folks. That's not what I do," he informed. He was an inmate too, so let the police be the police.

"I know that's right," the woman nodded at the correct answer. The last thing she needed or wanted was an inmate who acts like an officer. "This ain't Vegas but..."

"What happens in the chapel stays in the chapel," he finished to let her know they were on the same page.

"Welcome aboard, Stack!" She smiled and nodded at her new hire. A few interviews later she hired another vet called New York, because he was from New York. Now it was time to tend to some spiritual needs and do some anointing. "Next man!"

"Good morning ma'am, chaplain, ma'am," the thirty-ish black man stammered. He wondered if he came to the wrong place when she scrutinized him from head to toe before speaking. Seeing no signs of gayness she finally replied.

"Pull the door up and have a seat," she said and waited until he was seated. "Now, how can I help you?"

"I just, I mean, it's..." He stammered in search of the right words. Meanwhile the veteran chaplain was reading what was unwritten on his furrowed brow. She had been in the system long enough to speak the unspoken.

"First time in prison?" She asked and nodded without even reading his file.

"Yes ma'am. And it's, hard," he admitted. It seemed like a good idea to run credit cards but he hadn't counted on this part of the game. He should have, since prison is attached to any crime at any given moment. Hence the old adage, don't do the crime if you can't do the time.

"It is hard. Especially in the morning I bet?" She asked and wiggled her eyebrows. His head tilted, wondering if the old lady was making reference to the morning wood. That rock hard morning erection known as a piss hard on.

"Um, yes ma'am. I worry about my girl, can she wait two years? I worry about myself cuz these guys are, crazy!" He groaned.

There may be all kinds of people from all kinds of backgrounds and social classes, but there's only one chain gang. Everyone is lumped together with anyone else. The common denominator is violating Georgia law. Once your inside there only two species. Predator or prey.

"Let me see your dick," Chaplain Jordan remarked smoothly right in the middle of his moaning.

"And my mama is sick and she, excuse me?" He was saying until her words registered and stopped him mid sentence.

"You heard me. Pull that dick out," she said with a greedy smile. He didn't budge so she gave a little nudge. "If'n you don't, I'll call the CERT team and tell them that you did!"

The man had seen the dangerous group of men in

black beat many men on many occasions and wanted no parts of them. If showing the old lady the dick would save his ass he was all for it.

"It's not the biggest, but..." He sighed and whipped out the wood.

"It's pretty!" She smiled over her desk. "Get it hard!"

"Um, OK," he said and pulled his dick. The chaplain grabbed a bottle from her drawer and came around her desk.

"Some of my special anointed oil!" She explained as she squirted some on his dick. "Now work it in."

"Yes ma'am," he said and did just that. He was on autopilot from that point but still had a cheerleader.

"That's right, pull it. Tug, tug, tug, Mmhm!" She coaxed as he stroked. He put a little twist in his wrist with it but that was his idea. She saw his feet shift under him and knew it was getting good to him. "That's right! Release the demons! Release them dirty, nasty devils! Release in the name of...."

"Shit!" He grunted and skeeted on her desk and apologized for that and the curse. "Oops, my bad!"

"It's fine baby," she said and pulled a baby wipe from the dispenser. "Feel better?"

"Uh, actually I do," he nodded as he cleaned himself up. All his problems were still the same and his girl was already fucking but he did feel better for the moment.

"Good! So no reason to stick your thang in no man! No man mouth, butt or hand. You hear me?" She demanded.

"Uh, yeah," he grimaced since he had no intention on doing any of that anyway. He only had two years even though some guys fuck with two weeks. Only because what's already in them comes out of them. He wasn't gay so some time behind the wall wasn't going to make him gay.

"Send in the next man on your way out," she said just as casually as if she hadn't had the man jack off. There was a long line but she had plenty of her special anointed oil to go around.

"Clayton!" An inmate called out as he stopped from the counselors office. He had been hired on the spot as a counselor's aide and put right to work.

"That's me shawty," Trouble announced and stood. He entered the counselor's office and was waved over by a large lady tossing peanuts into her mouth every few seconds.

"Trevor Clayton?" She asked sparing him a slight glance from his thin file.

"Yes ma'..." He was saying before she resumed.

"You didn't put a work history?" She asked between and handful of peanuts and continued. "You ever work?"

"No ma'am. They put me in here for drugs," he replied but she missed the sarcasm. Most dope boys are dope boys because they don't have any other option.

Hunger is a hell of a motivator. Had there been jobs in the hood he would have gotten one to eat. There wasn't but there were plenty of junkies so he sold them drugs for the same reason, to eat. And while that's not a valid excuse, the other things missing from the hood were fathers and or role models to show them another way.

"Well, you finna become a dietary aide specialist!" She said as she assigned him to the kitchen.

"I was hoping to get my GED while I'm here?" Trouble asked since it would help him get out of there that much sooner. Let's hope the irony of getting a GED could have prevented him from coming to prison, and now helping him get out of prison doesn't go over anyone's head.

"That too!" She said and enrolled him in classes as well. She dismissed him by looking over him at her aide and announcing, "Send in Salaam!"

Trouble and Sa'id Salaam passed by each other with a cursory nod that acknowledged each others presence. He left the office while Sa'id took position in front of her desk.

"Still writing?" She asked as if he would stop. Making a living off your passion is the best job in the universe, why the fuck would he stop.

"Yes ma'am," he said and kept the sarcasm to himself. Its not always easy but he managed.

"Good. I'll just make you a teacher's aide so you can keep busy," she said, popped a peanut and called for the next inmate. D-Block was on its way to being staffed.

Chapter Eight

"Chow call!" Atkins called out and took count of the men filing past her. About half of the dorm went to mix and mingle even if they didn't eat the food. The handful of chicken nuggets were shaped like animals because they were the same ones served to preschoolers and daycare centers. In the same amount as well which adds to the chaos of prison. The powers that he would be better off if they fed the men properly so they could go lay their asses down somewhere. Instead they roamed around growling because their stomachs were growling.

"Y'all handle that," Rallo urged to his Rollers as he headed to the chow hall. Word of a civilian who smuggled in a cell phone had reached them and the Rollers take want they want when they want it. No contraband was flowing in yet so they were a hot commodity.

"We on it!" The youngsters said eagerly and rushed to carry out an armed robbery under the confusion of chow movement.

Prisoners can and will make weapons out of any and everything. They broke the plexiglass from an exit sign and sharpened the shards into knives. Most of the dorm went one way towards the chow hall while the three Rollers headed to the other dorm.

"See cuz on the fuck shit already," Trouble remarked when he peeped the movement.

"Shit, I hope them niggas try us! On god, I'll hit with anyone of them niggas!" Lil-Zay proclaimed. He had unfinished business with one so it was just a matter of when, not if.

"Yeah," Trouble sighed since mashing the button too was a matter of when. The Rollers were like a pack of wild hyenas. War was inevitable but he wanted to make as much money as he could before it popped off.

"As long as they keep the dumb shit out of here!" Stack protested. He was determined to keep the heat out the dorm. "Even animals don't shit where try eat shawty!"

"Them fuck niggas worse than animals!" Zay growled. He wasn't far from the mark.

The crew of Rollers waited until the Muslims, Mexicans and White boys left the dorm before they rolled in. No one wants drama in their dorm so they made sure no one was there to stop it. The rich civilian stayed back from chow call to handle some business. He had just pulled the phone from his hiding spot when the young boys ran in on him.

"You know what the fuck going on!" The first one shouted and stuck the man in his cheek.

"Y'all ain't gotta do it like this!" The man pleaded. He had enough money to buy plenty phones but no one sell new lives. He readily handed the phone over but the other two still stabbed him anyway. It ain't no fun if the crew don't get none so they commenced to wet his ass up.

The gentlemen hadn't been in D-Block twenty four hours yet before someone got killed.

"Are you kidding me? Tell me you're kidding me!" Mays demanded as she stomped her way to the crime scene.

"I wish I was," Davis moaned. They hadn't made a dime before logging their first murder. She waited with CERT team for her arrival.

"No one saw nothing right?" The CERT sergeant shouted up and around to the faces in the windows. Each man pulled away from the window when his gaze reached them.

"Yo mama did it!" Someone yelled from behind the locked doors. The man ran from door to door to see who said it but no one owned up to it.

"Warden on deck!" One of the CERT shouted when Mays clicked clacked her expensive heels into the dorm. Each clack reminded her how much money was at stake. Each clack made her more determined to get rich.

"Where is he?" She barked without bothering to release them from attention. They could stay like that if they wanted, she wanted to see the body.

"In here!" Davis said and waved to free the men from attention. They watched silently as she inspected the dead man. The punctures in his face and shoulder were harmless. One of the inmates have fixed those. The one in his chest poked his heart and took life.

"Damn shame! For a fifty dollar Walmart phone I bet," the warden said, shaking her head.

"Them phones be costing five hundred! Even more!" Her deputy corrected, wide eyed at the markup.

"Naw, they still fifty. Its the shipping and handling that cost five hundred," Mays laughed. The sergeant winced at the incongruous laugh over the dead body.

"Want us to shake the dorm down?" Sargent Quick asked eagerly. A little too eagerly for Mays who had other plans for the men in black.

"No. Go walk the perimeter," she dismissed. The CERT team had been sent here by the department so they weren't under her thumb, just yet. The best she could do was to keep them out of her way. Her mind was made up by the time they cleared the dorm her mind was made up. "Damn shame when they commit suicide."

"It is! Such a tragedy, "Davis agreed. She turned to the dorm officer and directed her next moves. "Call medical to collect him, then get your dorm ready for yard call."

"Good call, business as usual. Yard call, church call tonight. Tomorrow we get to work," the warden decided. She initially wanted to wait a week but knew the scarcer the contraband, the more violence over what little managed to get in. "It's time to flood this bitch!"

"White power!" Rabbit announced once his crew was all assembled. They had all paid for their drugs even if they had used them themselves. Not that Rabbit cared as long as he got paid.

"White power!" The minions repeated like a Trump rally. They were all pretty high though, just like a Trump rally.

"Look it," Ghost nodded towards Connor, while he was busy minding his own business. One of the most mysterious mysteries in creation was how someone minding their business bothered other people so much.

"Uppity cracker thinks he's better than us," Rabbit growled. In truth, Connor did have a better upbringing, better household, better parents and better education than the whole group of addicts put together, then multiplied but he was still in the same prison as them which made them even. Even still Rabbit was still jealous of the man.

"Yeah," Ghost cosigned since that's what men in his position do. The man next to the man merely echoes whatever the man says. Even if he wished he was Conner instead of himself.

They both watched as the handsome, blonde ran through a routine of exercises. The summer sun gave him a golden hue the pasty addicts envied. Once he finished his sets they set in motion to mind his business with him.

"Hey bud!" Rabbit greeted cheerfully and extended his hand.

"Sup guys?" Connor asked and squinted at his palm to make sure it was empty. He only had two years and had nothing to give and nothing to take. He eventually shook the hand but the second and a half delay was noted and considered a slight. Rabbit was shrewd enough not to show he was offended by the snub.

"Where you from?" Rabbit inquired casually.

"Look, your buddy already gave me your whole, 'white power' spiel, safety in numbers, niggers, spics, Jews speech. No offense, but I'm good. Just wanna do my few months here, off to work release and back home. If you guys don't mind? Please," Connor stated. He wasn't really asking, despite the question marks. He had spent time in the Fulton County Jail with those same niggers, spics, and Jews and got along with everyone. The black inmates separated themselves into gangs and cliques. They were so busy fighting each other everyone got a pass.

"Want me to stick him?" Ghost asked as if Connor wasn't present. He reached for piece of metal he pulled from the fence and sharpened to a deadly tip. This was as close to death as the near death overdose Conner experienced that cleaned him from the dope.

"For what? He's a white boy even if he isn't a White Boy! We'll always look out for each other," Rabbit said like the diplomat he had learned to be. In other words a prolific liar, just like disgraced ex president Trump.

"Yeah," Conner agreed and shook his hand. He really didn't agree but it let him get back to his work out.

"We really giving him a pass?" Ghost asked as they walked away.

"Hell naw! That cracker will get down if it kills him," Rabbit declared. The sting of the snub reverberated in his soul as they walked away. He was once prey until he became a predator. He saw the one who transformed him looking his way and stepped towards him.

"Wherw we going?" Ghost asked with a timbre of fear as they began towards the other gangs designated areas.

"We, nowhere. Go back to the group," he said over his shoulder as he left him behind. Rabbit ignored the taunts of 'cracker' and 'gringo' as he waltzed by the black gangs and the mixed Mexicans.

"Un-uh! Who this white boy!" Strawberry Shortcake hissed when he spotted the potential threat marching their way. The mixed group of sissies and men who liked sissies, known as The Bandos, all stood.

"He good," Dino said and waved them down as he stood. He stepped down from the bleachers and put his remaining eye on the one who took the other one.

"Dino," Rabbit greeted with a cursory nod. He had nearly three times as many White Boys staring over at them that were looking down at him.

"You looking good," Dino quipped and licked his lips. He always had a sense of humor for a booty bandit.

"How can you tell?" Rabbit shot back since he could be pretty witty himself.

"Touche!" Dino said once the disses were done. "What do you want?"

"Just to talk business. Personally I prefer to make money instead of war?" He replied and posed it as a question.

"I like money," he said in reply. Almost as much as he liked ass but knew Rabbit knew that first hand.

"Bring me back five hundred and we can do this every-day. As long as you bring me back five hundred," he said and produced a thousand dollars worth of meth in his palm. He was prepared to snap it closed if his head didn't nod. Just like it began to do.

"Hell yeah!" We ain't got no cream over where I am!'

He said. He could move this much just among his people. "How you want it?"

"Put it on the wire," Rabbit said and gave him the info. He tried to pretend he didn't feel One eyed Dino's one eye on his ass as he walked away. He did though and knew what he still needed to do. "I'm going to kill your ass!"

"We can get money, but I'm still going to kill your ass!" Dino mumbled as he watched the man walk off. "Might fuck him again first? Definitely going to kill him."

Chapter Nine

"*H*ole this down if you sure you don't wanna come," Stack offered even though he knew the answer. Church call was one of the few night time activities but Stack was the chapel aid so he had to attend.

"I ain't go to church on the street shawty, I'm pretty sure Ion wanna go in the chain gang!" He said and accepted the phone. He got to use it every day for a few minutes but now he could ride out a little bit.

"Check," he said and headed out the cell, out the dorm and over to the chapel area.

"Damn son, Chap packing them in!" New York gushed as the church service filled with men. He was surprised since the old lady mixed up the gospel with Motown hits. She might start with Luke but end up with Smokey.

"That anointment bring them out!" Stack laughed since he knew better. The chapel was another place where inmates from every side of the prison could converge for whatever. Even the perverted or nefarious.

The church service was to the prison drug trade what Memphis was to Amazon. A distribution hub that helped contraband flow through the prison. Most of that went straight over the old lady's head, since she was on the lookout for something else.

Homos might have boyfriends in another dorm on another side of the prison so this was one of the places they could hook up, besides the yard or details. Some would sit and hold hands while others took it a little further and gave each hand jobs while Chap read from the book of Barry. Gordy that is. Some took it a lot further and swapped blow jobs or butt fucked in the bathroom.

"Good evening gentlemen," Chaplain Jordan greeted once everyone was seated. They hollered back and she hit them with a, "god is good!"

"All the time!" The men chimed in and tuned her right out. She went on with her remixes while they handled their business.

"I know y'all wanna go home! I want y'all to go home too, but you gotta have patience. The patience of that man when he was in the belly of the fish. The patience he had when he was sitting on the dock of that bay. He didn't complain! No, he patiently watched the tide roll away!"

She was halfway through a Supremes hit when she spied one man ease off to the bathroom right after the another. The signs were posting for one man at a time, so two men was already a violation. The few men who were paying attention watched as she eased aside while harmonizing the chorus. She picked up a broom just before she entered the bathroom.

"Un-huh! You nasty devils!" Chaplain fussed as she

swung the broom. She caught one hung up in the other and went to swinging.

The group of men burst out uproariously as she chased them both out of the bathroom. Both had pants down around their ankles and couldn't outrun the old lady. She ran behind them whacking them both until the officer stepped in and cuffed them both. One was a Rider and the other a Roller, but both were caught.

"Can we at least pull our pants up?" The Rider griped after his hands were cuffed behind his back.

"Shouldn't have pulled them down!" The disgusted woman fussed and grimaced. She said used to write disciplinary reports when men masturbated in front of her but seeing the alternative changed her tune. From this night on she would ignore them and let them pull on their dicks until their heart's content. That was certainly better than this.

"What you got going on Bolo?" A Rider asked one of the men who got caught.

"Shit, I was fucking him! He wasn't fucking me!" He declared as if it made a difference who was fucking whom. Some homos were still in denial that pitching is better than catching. In baseball maybe, but its both gay otherwise.

"But I was finna fuck you after you finished! We been swapping out!" The Roller proclaimed to his crew in his defense. Either way Rallo and Trouble would hear about it.

"Daddy!" Malaysia cheered when she took the call. She had locked the number in already and knew who it was before picking up.

"Sup shawty," he cheesed. All that cool shit went out the window when he heard his baby coo and his baby mama's voice.

"You Ok?" You asked of the foreign entity in his voice. She couldn't identify it even though she heard it clearly.

"Who me? Oh, yeah. I'm good!" He replied quickly. The fresh murder in the other dorm weighed on him without even realizing it. She managed to take his mind off of everything else, if only for a moment. Meanwhile Rallo and company were enjoying the new phone.

"Damn she got a fat pussy!" One of the Rollers remarked of the porn star on the screen. They had just smoked a joint that JJ passed off from Dino. He was running up quite a tab already.

"Shit nice and meaty!" Rallo agreed of the beat up box. It was meaty like roast beef so he squeezed his erection through his pants. "I'm finna take a shower."

"I'll hold it down while you gone," his protégé offered and got laughed at.

"Shit, I'm taking this lil bih with me!" He announced and grabbed his toiletries. The young Roller just committed an armed robbery and murder to get the phone but had to wait in line. He might wanna rethink the whole 'big homie' and 'ride or die' thing but he didn't. Didn't think that is.

Obviously Rallo didn't think it through either. It could have worked out had he a plan, but he didn't. He held the phone in one hand and lathered his dick up with the other. He had a pretty good stroke going until the phone slipped. He tried to catch it with his dick hand but it was slick and slippery from the soap. The phone fell, cracked, sputtered and died.

"If worse come to worse," he shrugged and peeped through the hole in the shower curtain. It was brand new yesterday but several holes had been cut so the men could look at the female officers in the booth and jack off.

Just another day for the Gentleman of D-Block.

"How was work?" Malcolm asked his wife when she made it home from her first full shift with the inmates. They weren't even at capacity and they were already going crazy.

"I should be asking you that!" She snapped before she could catch herself. Not that it mattered since the concept had been lost on him. He had gotten comfortable living off his woman and would be no more good now. Like a race-horse with a broken foot, the best thing she could have done then was take him out back and shoot him. Put him out of his misery.

"Man I just asked how was work!" Malcolm fussed as if his sitting on his ass while she worked wasn't the problem. Or, if cheating with an old acquaintance was ok.

"How was work? Let me tell you how work was!" She shot back and filled him in. "First, I ain't never seen but your dick before today, but I seen at least a hundred! Every time I count, these men got they dick out. One managed to skeet as soon as I get to his room, every time! I ain't even know that was possible?"

"Man I..." Malcolm tried to cut in but Lalonda wasn't finished.

"Oh no! I'm finna tell you about my day! It wasn't just count time! These men shower with the curtain wide open just looking at me while jacking they dick! They was lined up all the way down the range. One was so bold he just came right up to the booth and masturbated right in front of me! My ole ass partner 'talmbout, just ignore them! Can you imagine, I'm literally being sexually assaulted and he said just ignore them! Then, these men fight all day. In and out the rooms just beating each other up..."

Malcolm huffed, puffed and blew his breath like he wanted to do something about the men disrespecting her. He would need to start with himself though he was disrespecting her the most by sending her up in the prison to pay their bills. For all his huffing and puffing, he never told her to quit. He needed to whoop his own ass.

"Just ignore them baby. Let me see the keys. I'm finna go for a drive," he said as if she didn't know where he was driving to. She did but didn't mind since it would get him away from her.

"Tell her to give you some gas money," she called after him. Lalonda was officially fed up and there was nothing he could do about it. She had ran out of love for her husband.

Chapter Ten

*M*alaysia was all smiles as she drove to the prison. Until she saw the prison that is. The brutal barb wire wiped the smile off her face in an instant. She shook it off as she parked and collected their baby from his seat.

She rocked a pair of skin tight jeans that hugged her curves like a Formula One car. The thong deprived the onlookers the satisfying trail of panty lines. The near sheer shirt hugged her heavy breast and showed off her perfect nipples. All eyes were on her as she approached but not just because she was a bad bitch.

"This must be yo first time visiting?" The officer asked when she reached the entrance.

"You would have known if you saw me before shawty!" She laughed, feeling herself.

"True! And you 'woulda knew you cain't come up in here like that," he informed. "You look good tho, just too good for here," he said and pointed at the posted dress code.

"Man I came all the way from Atlanta!" She moaned. She kept clothes in the car but they were too sexy for the prison dress code as well. "I gotta drive all the way home to change?"

"There's a dollar store in town," a woman behind her informed. She had learned this the hard way herself during the decade she had been riding with her man. Every prison had a dollar store nearby for situations just like this.

"Thank you," Malaysia huffed and marched off. Time came to a complete stop when all that ass got in motion. It didn't resume until she sat it back in the car. The seventy thousand dollar car got more attention than she intended.

"Seventy damn thousand dollars!" Davis announced when she googled the make and model.

"That's base! He's our man!" Mays corrected. They had a slow trickle of contraband coming in to keep the men sedated. Now it was time to mash the gas. They kept watch over the parking lot to see who was coming to see who and what they were driving.

"OK then," the deputy acknowledged when a customized SUV pulled in bearing a wrap featuring Sa'id Salaam book covers. The bright yellow truck did what it was designed to do and turned heads.

"Except he's not our guy," the warden moaned. He was known for his hustle but wouldn't touch anything forbidden. It had been a lifetime ago when he was dope boy. Now he just wrote dope books that sell like crack.

"Good thing he refused to be Imam," Davis cosigned. Jahil had several drug related disciplinary reports in his file so he would be the one to move their drugs using the Muslims as muscle. They wouldn't fight the flow, just tax it. They learned from Dre that everything went smoother when everyone was eating. Any imbalance could lead to war. No one wins in a war except the funeral homes.

Malaysia had her highly glossed lips twisted hard when she returned to the prison. The dollar store didn't have anything cute so she had to settle for what they had if she wanted to see her man.

If the prison was trying to reduce the amount of booty in the place the sweat pants Malaysia purchased only made matters worse. Now all that ass had wiggle room in the loose fabric, and wiggle it did. The baggy T-shirt down-played her chest but her backside was poetry in motion when she walked.

"Is this better?" Malaysia fussed when she returned to the entrance. The guard didn't answer as he registered her in for the visit. It wasn't until she and the baby cleared the metal detector did his see the booty bouncing around in the sweats.

"Shole is," he said and bit his lip.

"Clayton, Trevor. Visit!" The officer called through the intercom. Of course he knew that since he and Malaysia spoke most of the ride down from Atlanta. The Telsa did most of the driving so she was able to speak.

"Hit her with some of this!" Stack said and passed him a bottle of scented oil.

"This shit fiyah!" Trouble exclaimed when he took a whiff. He began dabbing on before asking, "What is it?"

"Sa'id Salaam! My boy who write the books got his own fragrance and err thing!" He laughed and shook his head.

"I showed him how to hustle when he first came in and he went crazy with it!"

"Put me in the game coach!" Trouble laughed again. He had already learned how to move in a dorm full of killers. An art, not for the faint of heart.

"I got you shawty. I'ma show you how to run the check up," Stack agreed as he left the room. He may have been out of the game but that didn't mean he couldn't coach.

Trouble felt at least a hundred individual eyes on him as he walked through the dorm. Some were nosey, others wished they were getting a visit. Prison is rough and sitting with loved ones for a few hours can smooth it out just a little. Meanwhile some others were just plain hating.

"He fucking our cousin!" Rallo said. Said it like he didn't pay his first cousin to fuck her. Then trick her into revealing their whereabouts so he could rob them.

"Shit, I'd fuck her if she was my cousin!" His young side kick Gip, acknowledged. Rallo had pulled her pictures off her social media to jack off to just to be spiteful. He wished he could have a bad chick like Malaysia holding him down. Nut's mother got in the wind the day after he got arrested. She got her son's car back and moved on.

Trouble walked into the large room used for visitation. It only took half a scan before he saw Malaysia's bright smile beaming brightly. Its mandatory to be as hard as possible in the dorms and on the yard but smiling was permissible in visitation. He matched her smile and walked over to embrace her.

"Hey daddy!" Malaysia cooed happily just like the happy baby in her arms.

"Hey 'yaself shawty!" He shot back before shoving his

tongue in her mouth. They twirled their tongues around for a moment like they used to do before they fucked. There would be no fucking today so they broke it off and smiled again.

"Here go yo daddy!" She sang to their child as she handed him over. The wattage of her smile increased as she watched father and child staring at each other for the first time.

"Lil Trevor! You ain't never finna be in here!" He vowed to his child on the spot. It hadn't been a week yet but more than enough to know this wasn't it. No amount of money is worth having men look up your ass or tell you to lift your sack so they can check under your balls.

"Clayton..." An officer called and motioned for them to sit. The state allows a hug and kiss upon arrival and departure. The inmate needs to be in his seat for the rest of the visit. The visitor is allowed to hit up the snack machines to feed them.

"I'm finna get you some food," she said and walked off with a bag of quarters. Her jiggling ass got a few men in trouble when she walked by. A few got popped or fussed at by wives or baby mamas for watching the wiggle and jiggle. Trouble was too busy bonding with his baby to notice.

Malaysia knew a few chicks who had rode a few bids with a few dudes a few times and learned the ropes. She grabbed up enough food to last the day instead of coming back and forth. Once the place filled up the machines would empty quickly. She grabbed burgers, chips, sodas and snacks as she went along. She only heated one of the burgers for now and held on to the rest.

"You not eating?" Trouble asked when she sat his food

in front of him but none for herself. The rest was piled under her chair for later.

"From a machine? Nigga I ain't got caught doing shit!" She laughed, then scrunched her face up at the food.

"Shit, me neither if not for punk ass Bama," he growled and bit into the burger. It needed ketchup but was still better the chow hall food. Commissary was coming Monday so he wouldn't have to eat in there anymore.

Malaysia watched him eat with muted amusement while searching for the words to tell him about the robbery that claimed everything they put away for the future. He looked up a few times while he chewed and sipped but waited until he finished eating in hopes whatever was eating her wouldn't spoil his appetite.

"Who is he?" Trouble asked after washing the last bite of burger down with the last sip of soda. She was young and fine and he was gone so he assumed the worst.

"Who? A nigga? Nigga you tripping!" She shot back fiercely. He almost got popped but the outburst got the guards attention.

"Man, something's up. Since I went to court. You been, different?" He said. He was in tune with her enough to see through the facade she built around the bad news. Ten years was a long time even with half off for good behavior.

"Cuz when I came home from court someone had broke in our apartment! Stole everything! Even clothes out the hamper!" She whined and finally had a good cry about it. Up until now it just pissed her off. Now it broke her heart.

"The money too?" Trouble asked and looked down at

his son. The curious face took some of the sting out of her answer.

"All of it. Even the damn jar of quarters," she moaned. "All I had left was what was on me. Plus a few hundred in the car."

"Hmph," he huffed since he needed time to think. The Telsa was leased but he still had the Caddy. It could go back if they couldn't afford it anymore. "Rent paid up?"

"Just for another month. I'ma hafta go back to the club!" She decided. "Shoot we still got a baby. You need money on yo books. We..."

"Naw shawty ain't no club!" He interjected. He wasn't crazy about her dancing before they started dealing with each other. That shit was definitely out now. The last thing he needed on his mind was her busting it open for random niggas, for money.

"But Trouble...."

"I said no! Now, if you single you can do whatever you want to do. If you with me, you not shaking your ass in niggas faces!" He snapped to whatever her but was. Obviously it was a but nothing because she zipped her lip.

"Real talk tho, that just made my pussy jump!" Malaysia whispered wickedly. Trouble just shook his head and laughed. Best case scenario was a few more years before he could watch her pussy jump. In the meanwhile he had to get his money up.

Chapter Eleven

"About dang time!" Trouble said when his name was called near the end of the commissary call. Stack had almost finished putting his food away before his name was called.

"Patience shawty," the vet reminded as he went to go get his food. That was his best advice since the chain gang required tons of patience if one wanted to retain ones sanity. After thirty years he would know better than most.

That newfound patience came into play real soon when he received twenty five dollars worth of food that cost seventy dollars in prison. Signing your name on that high priced receipt is a form of sexual abuse in itself. Like consenting to being molested or fondled.

"Here you go shawty," Trouble said, digging in the bag as soon as he came in the door. He was a firm believer in paying his bills and wanted to return the ten soups he had borrowed from Stack.

"That's you shawty. I already told you I don't loan shit. If I got it to give, I give. Loans are bad business," he advised and waved it off.

'A'ight then," he said and began to put his food away. His receipt said he could do this one more time before he was broke. Something had to give and soon.

"Pay day! Pay, mother fucking, day! Uh! Uh! Uh!" One eyed Dino cheered and did a little dance. Mainly just thrust his hips since he planned to fuck something. He turned down sexual favors from Honey Bun, Cupcake and the other food groups since arriving. He was saving it for someone special.

He ran a store that paid him two for one, three four two or five for three back. His money doubled and multiplied but was still cursed as interest is one on the most oppressive institutions on the planet. Some unlucky souls couldn't pay, so their bill doubled or multiplied again. Dino was smart enough to cash out a lot of the food he took in and converted it to real money in a bank account.

Some debtors got beat up every now and them to deter other debtors from running up tabs they couldn't pay. Dino would sic his crew of sissies on them to beat them publicly. Nothing is more humiliating than getting beat up by a band of punks. Others 'caught out' and checked into protective custody. Then others, like JJ wrote checks their ass would have to cash.

"Awe shoot! My Granny still ain't put my money on my books! I'ma have to call her again!" JJ fussed when his name didn't get called for commissary once again. It had been working thus far so he just kept on running it. Since he was so smart and all.

"Mmhm," Dino nodded in agreement. He owed two hundred dollars for phone time, food and weed at two for one. If he wanted to add to that, it was his ass. Plus Dino paid Rallo an ounce of weed to disown and disavow the former Roller. Now he was fucked, literally.

"Yeah, she be tripping. She old, Mmhm," he said. The truth was his granny wouldn't pee on him if he was on fire after all the things he stole out of her home.

"Shit, you may as well add another to yo tab?" Dino suggested as extended a thick stick of weed.

"Hell yeah!" He cheered. The most rhetorical of rhetorical questions is asking an addict if they want drugs. Of course they do and he snatched it from his fingers and lit it with the popper. JJ took a few greedy pulls before extending it back to share.

"OK den!" Dino laughed at the irony of sharing the weed that would cost him his ass. The day passed slowly since he was anticipating the big night.

There were plenty of sissies in the joint but Dino liked them fresh off the street. He loved the thrill of the hunt, and turning them out. That's how he evaded the deadly virus most chain gang sissies share and pass around from camp to camp. The majority of them were HIV positive, some with full blown AIDS. All of them were still fucking.

"Oooh girl my tummy hurt!" Cupcake groaned and clutched his six pack.

"Bitch all them different kids in there fighting!" Honey Bun howled. "Got black, Mexican, white..."

"Nuh-uh chile, Ion just drink err body water!" The man huffed indignantly as if being discriminating in which dicks he sucked was a virtue. It wasn't though, since he was a man and all.

"I'm finna take my shower. Y'all handle that," Dino said and stripped down to his muscular birthday suit. JJ had seen him naked so many times by now he thought nothing of it.

"We got you," Cupcake assured him as he stepped out of the cell. He used to head over to the shower butt naked until the Muslims politely threatened to kill him if he did it again. No one wants to finish prayer and come face to face with the next man's, mans 'ndem. He wrapped a towel around his waist and walked away.

"Handle what?" JJ asked and swooned from all the weed and liquor. He was high as a kite and that might help. Chain gang anesthetic to ease the pain heading his way.

"We got you," Honey Bun said and pushed JJ back on Dino's bed. He giggled as if they were real girls when they stretched his hands and feet out. The restraints were already in place making it easy to secure him.

"Y'all play too much!" He snickered when they began to strip him. Once he was naked he said, "quit playing!"

"You the one was playing!" Cupcake said and fondled him. He soon had a whole erection in his hand. "Mmhm."

"Knew he liked boys," Honey Bun added and grabbed the ointments. The two sissies rubbed him down with lotion and brushed his waves and got him pretty. Honey Bun had some free world lip gloss and polished his soup coolers. Cupcake used some Skittles and made his face up real pretty. They had him just right just before Dino arrived back at the cell.

"OK den! Got my bitch looking right!" Dino cheered. The sissies took their cue and took their leave.

"They play too much..." JJ was saying as Dino dropped the towel. He soon found out that no one was playing. Especially not Dino.

His next words were unintelligible gags and groans when the booty bandit mounted his face and pushed into his larynx. Tears streamed from his eyes from the oral invasion. Dino was literally growling as he pummeled his throat. Poor JJ almost choked, then almost drowned.

"Shit lil mama!" Dino grunted and grinded on his tonsils. "That's just the appetizer. To wet your whistle."

"That's fucked up!" JJ whined and wriggled under the restraints. "You ain't even have to do it like that!"

"No, what's fucked up is smoking and eating all my shit like you ain't gotta pay! So yeah, I had to do it like that!" Dino snapped. Plus he liked it like that. The squirms and moans helped get him off.

"No, I mean you ain't have to tie me up," JJ explained but Dino needed further explanation since he'd been gone so long. "You ain't have to take it. Bruh, I'ma two thousand baby. We been fucking!"

"Sho nuff?" Dino wondered as he undid the restraints. He had some attached to the top bunk to hold his legs in the air but may not have needed them from what he was saying.

"Facts! We twerk, suck dick, swap booty, all that!" He admitted to Dino's surprise.

"But, why?" Dino asked and strained to recall those days. He wanted some pussy real bad back when he was young but chicks didn't dig him. Now they love his dark, rugged good looks but it was too late.

"Prolly the drugs," he nodded. "We pop pills, sip syrup, smoke weed, lick molly, snort coke, shoot meth..."

"Well, damn?" Dino wondered. He liked to turn them out when they came in but they were coming in already turned out. "Well, no sense letting this hard dick go to waste."

"At all!" JJ purred and flipped over onto his belly. He didn't have much time to do but would do the rest of his time like that. His new name was Nutty Bar from then on.

JJ may have been having fun but for Merle, not so much. He had just returned to his cell with a net bag filled with a seventy dollar commissary when three young boys ran in behind him.

"Hey guys!" He greeted and produced a bag of Jolly Ranchers to share with them.

"Nah dad, come off that sack!" One said and snatched the entire bag of food. Another took an empty net bag to his locker and stole everything worth stealing. He scooped up all of his hygiene items, stationary and stamps. Even books they would never read just so he couldn't have them. The other took his tennis shoes, slippers and shower shoes. They left him as bare as when he arrived from the county. Except for the promise to be back next week.

Well, they did come back week after week until times got desperate so he sought out desperate measures.

"Been waiting on you!" Dino said when the child molester arrived at his cell. He sought protection from the Muslims first but got shot down. They were a religious group, not gang, not protection agency.

Next he tried the Rollers since they were the ones robbing him. He paid them once but they just robbed him again. Going to the Rollers first got him chumped off by the Riders and the Mexicans only looked out for themselves. The only ones left were the Bandos.

"Huh me? Oh, Ok," he stammered and got back to business. "Yeah, I um need um..."

He was stuttering and stammering but Dino cut to the chase and whipped out the wood while he was still speaking. The predator liked little boys but still started down at the grown man dick.

"Excuse me," Nutty Bar said and hopped up from the bed. He rushed from the room just before the predator was turned into prey. Dino forced himself on and in the man as soon as he left. The sounds of the rape reverberated around the dorm but no one cared.

"Whew weeeee!" Dino grunted at the conclusion of taking his virginity. They say it ain't no fun when the rabbit got the gun and they were right. Merle grunted and grimaced from the same abuse he heaped on young boys.

"So, you'll, protect, me!" Merle panted once the man slumped over on his back.

"Sure. You just gotta finish paying," he said as he pulled

from his colon and went to the sink to wash up. Honey Bun and Cupcake walked in and pushed him back on the bed. The two HIV positive men took turns raping him next. And it still cost him sixty dollars a week in store goods just to keep the remaining ten. It was better than nothing, yet more than he deserved for messing with kids.

Chapter Twelve

"**S**tand by for inspection!" The dorm officer shouted sounding scared. She scrambled to get her own area and log books in order while the inmates moved at a leisurely pace.

There wasn't enough contraband around to smoke up the dorm so no one needed to wipe down. Inmates live under the fallacy that wiping bleach all over the walls kills the smell of weed and tobacco smoke. It doesn't. A non smoker will clearly smell bleach, weed and tobacco smoke.

"Shit! These folks got me stuck down here," Stack fussed when he was stuck in the dorm for inspection. He usually got to miss the warden's inspections by being at detail.

"What all she finna do?" Trouble asked since this would be his first. The administration let them breath the first week to get adjusted but now it was time to get down to business. In more ways than one.

"Shit, walk through, sniff the air, check for black eyes, make sure beds made, locker box neat," he explained.

Trouble turned to readjust his locker since he didn't want any smoke. The warden, deputy warden and the inspection team entered the area and the men scrambled to line up beside their cells. Shirts tucks, Crocs crocced, pants pulled above their waist and hair cut.

"Warden on deck!" The dorm rep shouted as the inspection team entered the unit.

"Ma'am, good morning ma'am. Dorm ready for inspection ma'am!" The men all shouted in perfect positions of attention.

The vets had already explained that wardens take the sound offs seriously. It was a sign of respect one way or the other. A loud sound off could turn a vain warden around at the door. The flip side was a weak sound off could get the dorm shook down, locked down or commissary lost for the week. The inmate who refused to sound off and got the dorm in trouble may as well leave with the inspection team or get their ass whooped once the inspection team left.

"OK then!" Mays nodded and smiled at the thunderous greeting. It gave her vagina a slight quiver and reminded her she needed some dick as well as some money. The old chaplain used to tighten her up before, but now he was gone.

Warden Mays hit the downstair cells while deputy warden headed up the stairs. She put a little extra on her walk to divert attention to her ass and away from the bag in her hands.

"Mmhm. Ok. Nice job. Line your shoes," Davis said as she went along each cell. When she reached Stack and

Troubles she swerved and went inside. Both stood at attention in the doorway while she went into each locker box. A minute later she came out a little lighter than she went in. "Nice job Clayton."

"What was that about shawty?" Trouble asked through clenched teeth like a ventriloquist since the inspection team was still there.

"We finna see," Stack whispered back. He had seen it before and had an idea.

"Good job men!" Warden Mays said as she headed out. She made sure to make eye contact with Trouble when she did. She twirled her fingers in a circle, meaning to 'carry-on' as she left the dorm.

Trouble and Stack bumped into each other as they both rushed into the room. Stack was bigger and won that battle. Trouble was right behind him and pulled his locker box open. He blinked at the black plastic bag laying on the middle shelf. It wasn't there before so it was no mystery where it came from.

"Let me put the flap up shawty!" Stack exclaimed since he knew what was going on. Nosey niggas loved to walk around the dorm looking in cells to see what they could see. Some were just nosey, others looking for some contraband to buy or beg. Others were the police who ran and told the police everything they saw. Once the 'nosey nigga' flap was up Trouble pulled the bag out and laid it on the desk. He hesitated for as second before opening it. "Scared, say you scared!"

"My bad!" Trouble said when he unfroze. He opened the bag and found a tightly wrapped package of weed. Then a bag of tobacco, followed by several cell phones. He was stuck on the contraband so Stack picked up the note with instructions.

"Cash app info. She said she want three thousand back off this," Stack read and looked at the work. His head nodded at the nice profit to be made but Trouble couldn't see it.

"Three racks! For this!" He grimaces like the idea stunk. He weighed the weed with his touch and knew it was a half pound compressed. He subtracted one on the cell phones for himself and slid the other four aside. He didn't know what to think of the can of tobacco.

"Shawty! You can get a stack off an ounce. Another stack each for the phones and at least six hunnid for the tobacco!" The vet broke down. Those were just the wholesale prices with plenty meat left on the bone for the next man to eat too.

"We on!" Trouble announced wide eyed with wonder. He had been wracking his brain trying to come up with a come up and one fell right in his lap.

"You on shawty" Stack corrected. "I'll show you how to move and send some folks your way, but this you. Any heat, be twenty one about it."

"Fa sho!" Trouble agreed since he was definitely twenty one about his. He was in here because a man couldn't be twenty one about his and snitched on everyone else.

"Let me go get this hook," Stack said and went to the 'put-up man'.' This was the man tasked with finding or building a spot to hide phones and other contraband. A good 'put-up man' is worth his weight in gold. He's often part magician who can make a spot in plain sight that the administration and CERT team can't see. He charges by the week and can make as much money as the spot can hold.

Most smart people never hide their phone in their own cell. If they lose it in the spot at least it can't be put on them. The reckless ones keep them in their locker box and hope not to get caught.

Getting a phone in prison is just one part of the battle. Keeping it can be several battles in itself. Most civilians need not even get one if they're not connected or paying for protection. Because the broke gang bangers will rob them. The few civilians like Stack and others who were built like that didn't have that problem.

Still, they had to stay on point and not get caught slipping. Most things can be prepared for but the 'humbug' is not one of them. The humbug is not an insect but can be just as pesky. One slip up, one falling asleep with the phone in hand, one talking too loud, can get you knocked off.

"Let me hit a few of my folks..." Stack said when he returned with the phone. Trouble had already began breaking the work down to spread out. He pushed a little aside to smoke, then pushed it back.

"Business before pleasure," he said to himself as Stack worked the phone. A few calls set things in motion and they sold out in minutes.

"What's the cash app shawty?" Stack asked. The vets who had phones were ready to buy everything on the spot while they could.

"Troublegirl21," he said and gave Malaysia's info. Stack relayed the info and the money started rolling in. "I better call her."

"Here Jone," Stack said and passed it off. A curious Malaysia answered on the first ring.

"I just got five thousand dollars on my cash app?" She fussed like it was a problem.

"Send three racks here..." He said and read off the info Warden Davis left. "Hold on to the rest!"

"What you got going on?" Malaysia wanted to know as she did what she was told. "Matter fact, Ion even wanna know. Just keep doing it!"

"I'm is!" He assured her. The sales left a little left over for him to celebrate. He set a little of that aside to keep the peace.

"Knew he was the right one!" Davis mumbled to her boss as they were still inspecting. They had made more drops but each group got a different cash app so she knew it was Trouble who paid off.

"Are you kidding me?" Mays reeled and laughed. They had definitely picked the right one in trouble. Meanwhile he was on his peace keeping mission back in his dorm.

"Sup cuz?" Trouble asked as he tapped on the frame of Rallo's door. The room was full of young Rollers glaring back.

"Come on in!" Rallo invited but Trouble wasn't feeling it. If one of the young boys said anything slick he would go straight in their mouth. He knew Zay and the other Riders had eyes on him and would come running. Being in a gang war could cost him from going home early so he planned to avoid it at all cost.

"I'll just holla at you later," Trouble said and turned to leave, knowing full well his cousin wouldn't let him.

"Y'all spread out for a lil minute so I can holla at cuz," Rallo dismissed.

"We right out here," Gip said looking Trouble up and down as he walked by. Trouble just laughed at the kid but knew he would be the one. Just like a toddler doesn't understand the word hot, until he burns himself. Gip wouldn't understand the word trouble until he got in trouble.

"Anyway, I came up on a lil something so you know I gotta look out," he said and passed Rallo some free weed. Rallo blinked and scrunched his face at it for a second as if it wasn't enough. Enough, free weed.

"Shit, fuck with me if you catch a plug 'fo I do," he said as he accepted the free weed. Trouble tried to hold his tongue but felt the words bubbling up anyway. The best he could was sugarcoat them a little.

"Remember what happen last time I fronted you some work?" He asked so he could convict himself. The right to remain silent applied but Rallo never could keep quiet.

"What? When? Nothing happened?" He replied.

"Exactly," Trouble said and walked out. He glared at the youngin who was playing with matches. He could get the smoke now if he wanted but the kid turned away.

"Tripping about a funky lil six 'hunnid funky ass dollars," Rallo moaned because he remembered exactly what happened. He tricked the money off, then stole it back to trick again. He put his flap up so he could smoke without his team while Trouble blazed with his. Proof that there's levels to this shit and Trouble was a leader on another level.

Chapter Thirteen

"Sup," Rabbit offered along with a Styrofoam cup of black coffee as he sat in front of the TV.

"I don't want any problems bro," Connor said and raised his hands in surrender. He usually stayed in his cell reading or writing but wouldn't miss the news.

"It's coffee, no problem," Rabbit assured him and tried again. Conner looked skeptical so Rabbit switched the cups and offered the one he sipped from.

"Thanks," he sighed and accepted the offer.

"What's going on in the world?" Rabbit asked as if interested. He lived in the here and now so he didn't worry much about what went on the other side of the wall. If it wasn't coming into the prison it didn't concern him.

"Biden pulling the country out of the hole that clown Trump put us in," Connor sighed. He missed Rabbit flinch at the dis of his god

. . .

Demigod and went on. Rabbit stayed focused on his main mission and let it go for now. For now he nodded and went along with everything they said.

"You're alright!" Rabbit declared after the small talk was cut short by the approach of the inspection team.

"You're not so bad yourself," Connor nodded in agreement. He would never invite the man home around his family but coffee and the news was ok.

"Catch you in the morning? I'll bring the coffee," he offered and was accepted.

"Sure," Connor agreed and went to stand by his cell for inspection. Moments later the officer opened the door and in walked the wardens.

"Warden on deck!" The dorm rep shouted.

"Ma'am, good morning ma'am! Dorm ready for inspection!" The dorm hollered back.

"Good morning men!" Warden Mays greeted back and began her inspection. This time she took the top range while her deputy handled the bottom range. Rabbit's cell was on the end and was the first one she went in.

"Bottom bunk!" Davis called out to the men standing at attention.

"Ma'am?" Rabbit asked and presented himself.

"What is this?" She asked of the lump under his blanket.

"Ma'am, I don't know ma'am," He said and squinted down at it. He knew when she pulled it back to reveal the contraband she placed there. "How much? How you want it?"

"I need three back on this, but let's say..." She paused to

come up with a number good for everyone involved. "Let's say five grand a week on your other operation."

Rabbit blinked, paused and thought. For her to be here and say what she said, meant she knew more than he could deny. Officer McCoy followed him from his last prison to keep the flow of drugs flowing. Five thousand was certainly reasonable for what he was making so his head gave a nod. Plus he had the meth operations all to himself at the moment.

"Five grand it is!" He agreed and accepted her payment info.

"That's for this, but hit this number if you need some pussy. I know you white boys love some black sugar!" She laughed and hit with the info for **PBTB**. Rabbit nodded like he agreed but hadn't had any color pussy in his life. He drifted away into his mind and wondered about the feel and taste of an actual vagina. If it was anything like the 'fe-fe' the men made he wanted in.

"What was that about?" Officer McCoy asked as soon as the inspection team cleared the dorm.

"The green light!" He cheered as he dug out the phones, weed and tobacco. As is stood he had the meth market to himself. It was only a matter of time before the other factions found a way in but he was the man for now. Now that some contraband had hit the camp the money would start flowing.

"Prime me up lil mama," Dino ordered when the officer announced the arrival of the inspection team. Nutty Bar dipped down and did what he was told. Partly because he was told but also because he liked to. It may have something to do with the skinny jeans but a lot of these dudes liked dick. Dino liked that just fine.

Dino also liked to stand on line for inspection with a nice, rock hard erection for inspection. He loved the looks the women gave at all that good meat, going to waste. He spied a few male staff eying the wood like a woodchuck and let them know he saw them.

"Warden on deck!" Lalonda shouted at attention.

"Ma'am, good morning ma'am!" The dorm replied as loud as they could to get them out of there as fast as they could.

"Ok then," Davis chuckled at Lalonda still propped up at perfect attention. She snapped out of it and fell instep with her. "Un-uh sis. With the warden."

"Yes'm ma'am," she said and rushed over to Warden Mays's side.

"Whose room is..." Davis was trying to ask when she reached the cell Dino and JJ shared. She knew full well who was assigned there but the long lump of dick in his britches threw her for a loop.

"That's ours," JJ said with a knewfound lisp to go with the limp. Both courtesy of that same lump in Dino's pants. He was developing an overbite from the same thing.

"Well damn!" She said and she noticed his arched brows and glossy lips. Her mission suddenly came back to her and she stepped inside the cell while waving Dino in as well.

"You must wanna see this dick?" He asked since many did.

"You must not wanna get no bread?" She shot back and produced the product.

"Hells yeah!" He said and readily accepted the contraband. He quickly stuck it into JJ's locker box until after inspection.

Vets always keep a fall guy to fall on the grenade and take a charge for them. Usually short timers like JJ who didn't have to worry about parole. They were going home anyway so there was nothing they could do to them. Mays turned to leave but an afterthought stopped her in her tracks.

"Matter fact, I do wanna see it," she asked looking at his crotch. He whipped it out and wagged it around for her. Her head shook from side to side with the dick, "Damn shame. What a waste!"

"Oh, it ain't going to waste honey chile," JJ lisped all sassy. He planned to finished what he started the second they cleared the dorm. These two thousand babies are something else.

"You got some money?" Bessie asked when she saw an inmate eying her big body. She was promised both money and dick by Davis if she came and worked at the prison. So far all she did was work. "Cuz you looking mighty hard!"

"Hell yeah!" He cheered. They may have forced him to work the kitchen for free but he still had some money to come home to.

"Two hundred and you can get some of this pussy," she explained. The man's eyes went wide at the prospect of at the offer. It was her pussy but she had to split the money with Davis since it was her hustle.

"How you want the money?" He asked and went for his zipper.

"Slow down big boy!" She said and grabbed his dick through his pants. She used her free hand to scribble her payment info. He had a choice to do Cash App, Venmo, PayPal or Western Union.

"I'll be right back!" He shouted and headed out the kitchen.

"Hold on inmate!" The officer assigned to the kitchen ordered before he could get away. He knew inmates had a history of stealing food to make sandwiches to sell in the dorm. He didn't knock the hustle but those sandwiches were good as fuck and he wanted one.

"Ion even got nothing!" The inmate moaned. He was trying to go pay for this pussy and dude was in his way.

"On the wall then!" The officer demanded and began to pat him down. He went a little too far up his leg and ended up with dick in his hand. He fell away and turned red from embarrassment.

"Mmhm, told you!" He laughed and rushed off. He made it to the dorm and retrieved his phone from the hiding spot. He shot her the money over the wire and rushed back to his detail.

The kitchen officer was still embarrassed about touching the man's dick when he returned. He turned his head as he rushed back through and found Bessie where he left her.

"You got that?" He asked excitedly when he reached her.

"Mmhm!" She giggled girlishly. Bessie didn't get much dick on the street so she jumped at Warden Davis's offer to sell pussy by the pound. Not literally by the pound since she was closer to three hundred than the two hundred dollars she charged.

The inmate dropped his pants and produced a quivering, rock hard erection. Big Bessie's box was bubbling hot when she saw the dick and rushed to get out of her pants. A pallet of blankets was laid out behind some boxes so she laid out and spread her thick legs.

"Fuck it!" He thought and dove face first into the plump vagina. After five years without pussy he wanted to a taste.

"OK then!" Bessie cheered as she got her first taste of oral sex. She had a few late night drunken dicks but no one ever ate her. She didn't last a good three minutes before her rolls got to rolling from a good nut. He rushed up to shove his dick in while she was still shivering but she slowed him up by retrieving a rubber from between her big breast. "Hmp!"

"Oh yeah!" He said like he forgot even though he had every intention in running up in that fat pussy bareback like a rodeo cowboy. He rolled the rubber down and squeezed into her tight vagina. She came quick but he came quicker with a variety of grunts and fuck faces. "Shit! Fuck! Argh!"

"I know right!" Bessie giggled again. She knew she wasn't the prettiest and knew she was overweight and out of shape, but she also knew she had some bomb pussy.

"Damn you got some good pussy!" He confirmed what she already knew. "Can I go again?"

"I'm supposed to charge you again," she remembered. She sold pussy by the pound but got paid by the nut. The idea of rejecting the good, stiff dick already up in her didn't appeal to her in the least. She gripped his hips and said, "Come on with it!"

He came on with it and lasted twice as long as the first. Still in all he spent two hundred dollars in under ten minutes. The big girls were a gold mine. Especially since men gossip more than women. He told one person who told two people who told two more people and **PBTP** was on the map.

Chapter Fourteen

*T*he driver pulled to a stop at his destination but didn't tell his passenger. She offered him a blow job for the ride and she was still on the clock. Her shift was coming to an end when his legs shifted underneath him.

"Shit shawty!" He cussed like good head with make you do.

"Mmhm," Reecie hummed and threw her neck into overdrive. She felt his satisfaction pulse into her mouth as he writhed above. She was still young so she opened the door and spit the kids on the curb. "You gonna wait for me?"

"Mmhm, hell yeah!" He lied convincingly. He was already in trouble for staying out all night and had to go face his baby mama. One of the pitfalls of living with a chick is getting evicted at the drop of a dime.

"Awe man!" Reecie moaned when he pulled away before she made it two steps away from the car. She had been in and out, sticking and moving in the wee hours ever since Malaysia got on her ass. The Telsa was no where in sight so she relaxed a little as she traipsed towards the house. She had time to wash her ass, change her clothes and snap a few pictures of her baby to post like a good mama.

'Wack' said the smack that made a spark in the predawn darkness.

"Un-huh! Got yo ass now!" Malaysia announced after jumping out of the bushes. She took Reecie down with a leg sweep and put her weight on her.

"Mmhm!" Granny hummed knowingly since she was old enough to know you can run but you can't hide. She had been watching her abandoned baby since she ran off but didn't mind since she had been raising abandoned babies for decades. She named them all cousins whether they shared the same blood or not.

"Go on and whoop me then!" Reecie dared and lifted her chin.

"Oh, I'm finna whoop you!" Malaysia assured her, but had a question first. "Why? Why you help set us up to get robbed?"

"I didn't! I had Rallo drop me to the Wendy's and walked from there!" She vowed and dropped a genuine tear. "On god I ain't know he was gonna follow! I would never set you up!"

Malaysia paused to reflect on the human waste named Rallo. She recalled him stealing her money, sniffing her panties and busting in the bathroom while she showered. She didn't know about how he would sneak in their room and jack off on the girls as they slept.

"Man..." Malaysia moaned and got up. She didn't help her up, but didn't whoop her ass either.

"Man..." Granny moaned too and stopped recording since there would be no fighting. "Now you need to get in here and see to your baby!"

"Wash yo mouth out before you kiss him. I 'seent you sucking that man dick!" Malaysia cackled.

"Shoot he ate my pussy in the room last night," Reecie bragged. "In the VIP room, and again at the motel!"

"What VIP room?" Malaysia reeled. She had been stalking the house for a week and wondered why she couldn't catch her.

"Shoot you know I'm dancing now! Just like you!" She sang proudly while Malaysia felt in the opposite direction. It's good to be looked up to for but she didn't want anyone following her footsteps that led to a strip club.

"You gotta be careful in them VIP rooms!" Granny said, shaking her head. Her granddaughters whipped their heads in her direction, wondering what she knew about that life. "Y'all heifers think they just started strip clubs? Shit, cave women were 'bussing it open back in they day!"

"Ion even wanna know granny!" Malaysia said and pulled Reecie into the kitchen. She knew there was no turning the girl down after getting turned on to the easy money, drugs and alcohol. Handsome, rich men actually paying her for sex is not something the girl would stop just because she said stop. Stop and do what exactly? So the best she could do was advise.

"I know, I know. Make them niggas wear a rubber!" Reecie sang exasperated as if she heard it a hundred times. She had and still had a baby so Malaysia had other advice.

"That too but stack yo bread! Get your money and put it up!" She warned. She wished someone had given those jewels to her when she was dancing. Instead she tricked off a bunch of money on ridiculous looking clothes and shoes just because they were trendy. Then, when she got wiped out by the robbery she realized just how much value that stuff had. She couldn't eat it or feed it to her baby.

"Un-huh! That's what I'm finna do! Right after I get me some Yeezies and some Breezies and..." The young girl said with stars in her eyes. The classic definition of in one ear and out the next. Unfortunately the best learned lessons are learned the hard way.

"Chile..." Malaysia sang and sighed. It was what is was and will be. She was just happy Trouble was both staying out of trouble and sending money home daily.

"Yo girl Laquanda be showing me what's up! She said y'all was tight!" Reecie happily reported.

"Tight hell!" She replied with a eye roll. She was still hot about her and Trouble but kept it to herself.

"Oooh! Oooh! Guess who I seen at the club! Tryna get me to suck his thang at the table! I was like boy you better pay for a VIP room! I ain't finna suck no nigga dick at the table!" Reecie declared her high standards for sucking dick.

"Who?" Malaysia asked and left the rest of that alone. What she wasn't going to do was try to guess who, from the whole city of Atlanta was in the club.

"Shawty who used to be with Trouble 'ndem. That nigga they call Bama...."

∾

"Sho nuff!" Trouble said when Malaysia delivered the good, albeit late news on their nightly video chat. Had they had Bama's whereabouts before they took their pleas they wouldn't have had to take their pleas. He would be in a box like Ridell just like the case against him.

"So, what you want me to do?" She asked, ready to carry it herself if need be.

"Nothing. Don't do nothing. I'ma let my Riders handle that," he said since he was king. That should have been that on the matter so he switched to other matters. "Let me see something..."

"What you tryna see!" She fussed as if she didn't know. She knew that's why she had it shaved and shining for him.

"Quit playing with me!" He laughed and she quit playing and pointed the phone between her thick legs.

"This what you looking for?" She asked as she parted her lips to impart some pink on him. It was already plump and glistening from excitement so she slid her finger inside with a hiss. "It's so tight!"

"I know it is," he said and shook his head at the memory of her vice like box. A C-section kept it like that after the birth of their child and he couldn't wait to squeeze back inside of it.

"Oooh you make, me, sick!" Malaysia moaned like it was his fault she was about to come. All he did was talk dirty to her while she made circles of her swollen clit.

"You wanna come for daddy! Go on and come!" He coaxed as his bunkmate walked into the room.

"I'll be back," Stack said and backed out when he heard the moans coming through the line.

"Ok baby, you win. I'll come!" She screeched and bust a good nut. It was good but she still wanted some dick.

"Mmhm," Trouble laughed as she made fuck faces and writhed.

"Make me sick!" She pouted at his laughing at her. Once she recovered they moved back to small talk about the big money rolling in. It wasn't much compared to when he was home but he wasn't home. Still he reversed the flow of dough. Most inmates had people sending money into the chain gang. He was sending money out.

"Aight shawty. My bunkmate back from detail. He need the room," Trouble said to say goodbye. It was actually a see you later since they would text more tonight as well as see each other this weekend.

"Ok baby. I need to go wash all this honey off my fingers," she purred but licked them instead.

"You so nasty!" He laughed and clicked off. He stepped outside the cell and gave Stack a nod to indicate he was clear. Then went back to grab a couple of sticks to smoke with Zay while letting Stack get the room.

"Sup Jone," they greeted in passing as he headed over to Zay's cell. His head shook at the heavy weed smoke in the air. Night shift was now hit or miss since the rookies changed to nights. Rallo didn't care, he was ball til you fall since getting put on by the wardens as well. Trouble knew what they knew and it was just a matter if time until he fucked up their money.

Chapter Fifteen

"There he is!" Connor cheered when Rabbit appeared with their morning coffee. He actually began to enjoy his company since Rabbit had questions about everything and he liked talking about everything.

"And here's Joe!" Rabbit sang as he sat the cups on the chair between them. He always let Connor chose which cup he wanted to drink from to show he could be trusted.

"Thanks," he said and chose the one closest to him as a sign that he trusted him. They looked back up at the TV as the reporter talked about the recent insurrection at the Capitol. "Would you look at these yahoos!"

"Crazy huh?" Rabbit agreed even though his heart yearned to be in the fray along with those yahoos. Rabbit didn't know a capitol from a capital but did love him some Trump. Little did those yahoos know, Trump despised the same country bumpkins who adored him enough to carry out an insurrection at his behest.

"Fucking, vanilla isis!" Connor cracked and cracked up

at his own job. Rabbit snickered along but didn't find it funny. He did smile inwardly as Connor took big slugs of the coffee. Ghost and the others always pouted when he spent time with the uppity white boy who looked down on the White Boys. Rabbit claimed he had a plan but it seemed like he enjoyed their morning ritual.

"Vanilla Isis, I get it!" He laughed and watched as Connor drained the last of the coffee with a satisfying slurp.

"Yeah, they're all gonna end up..." Connor was saying when a strange feeling began to creep through his whole soul. A feeling he knew so well but it was strange to feel it again after giving up drugs for so long. The unmistakable euphoria could only come from one place. "You son of a bitch!"

"Something wrong Connor?" Rabbit sang with a shit eating grin. His patience had paid off and his plan had worked. He rocked his victim to sleep and slipped him a hefty dose of methamphetamine in the coffee.

"Bruh I was fucking clean for almost a year! I can't believe you did this" Connor fussed as his soul pushed and pulled. He both hated and loved the feeling coursing through his body. He only quit after drugs claimed the life of his friend and cost him his freedom. He'd get his freedom back in a matter of months but his friend was never coming back.

"Yeah well I did!" He shot back and stood like a dare. Connor may have been taller, and more athletic but Rabbit was a White Boy and the Rest of the White Boys were watching. "What you gonna do about it?"

"This..." Connor replied and knocked Rabbit smooth out. A solid shot to his chin dropped him right back in the seat he just rose from. He looked like he had fallen asleep watching the TV.

"Hey!" Ghost barked in disbelief as his leader went down. He led the charge of White Boys to confront Connor, but Connor was with the shits.

"Bring it on you fucking crackers" he dared and ripped his T-shirt off like the hulk used to do. He was a deep tan instead of green but ripped and muscular from his daily work outs. Not to mention the dose of meth running through him.

Meanwhile the White Boys were pasty meth addicts who laid around the dorm getting high and eating. Some hadn't been to sleep in days and needed a nap. They were about to get some well needed sleep. The first two that reached Connor got laid out like toddlers at nap time. Ghost and two more engaged him in a fist first and got as much as they gave. The three on one seemed like a fair fight until Ghost upped the ante and upped the banger.

"Coward," Sa'id remarked to himself when Ghost stuck Connor from behind. Connor managed to block the blade and only got hit in his arm. He wisely retreated and put a table between himself and the knife.

"They ever try us, we finna eat on they ass!" Samir said from his side. The white Muslim brother loved to fight but, Sa'id kept silent and nodded internally.

Luckily for Connor or the White Boys the cops came running into the dorm when they saw the knife play. They don't mind a fist fight when it's a one on one but when it's a gang bang or weapons they come running. Sa'id knew what was coming next and turned to his cell. He had plenty of books to read or write to keep him busy.

"Lock it down!" The officer shouted and banged the table with his stick. The dent it put in the stainless steel was a deterrent to any of the young boys who didn't want to comply. Conner was lucky officer McCoy wasn't working today or that would have been his head with the dent in it. Instead he was taken to medical to get a few stitches.

"Nap time at the daycare?" Deputy Warden Davis quipped when she arrived on scene. Rabbit and the others were still sleeping soundly around the TV.

"Fucking white boy can fight!" The officer admitted. He missed the first knock out but watched Connor go toe to toes with five men.

"Move him to another dorm," Davis ordered so he wouldn't get murdered. Not for his sake but her own. The White Boys were doing numbers with the meth and didn't want a murder to mess it up.

The lockdown lasted a few minutes until they could pack Connor's belongings and move him to another dorm. He was probably going to have problems from the White Boys in whatever dorm he landed but it wouldn't be this one.

"Should we wake them up?" The officer asked since Rabbit and the other two were still sleeping soundly.

"Naw, let em sleep," Mays said since they were snoring and drooling. She knew the meth heads stayed up for days at a time and figured they needed some rest.

Sa'id heard the doors open and the dorm fill with chatter but was engrossed in a book. One can never get enough reading about the greatness of Allah and His majesty so he just kept on reading. He would have kept on reading if not for a tap on his door. He looked up expecting one of the good brothers with a good question. He loved when they came to him with questions he could answer but particularly loved the ones he couldn't answer. Because those required him to do some study and learn more. Then the blessings of teaching it to others. It wasn't any of them but a civilian from the dorm.

"Yeah?" Sa'id called and waved him inside.

"Hey, um yeah, how I can be a moozlim?" He asked since his mind was made up. He had decided on the way down in the van with Trouble but waited to see if it was going to be necessary or not. Things started slow but D-Block was getting rougher by the day.

"I don't know," Sa'id replied and turned back to his book. That was body language for 'beat it'. Dude obviously didn't speak that though and stuck around.

"But, ain't you a moozlim?" He asked in confusion. Not only did he see Sa'id with the others but he lead the congregational prayers in the dorm and took turns giving the Friday sermons with Jahil.

"No, I am not. I am a Muslim," he corrected and sat the book down since he knew more was to follow.

"Oh Ok den. I wanna be a Muslim. What I gotta do?" He fixed and asked. He saw the new gang bangers get beat in all the time and hoped it didn't take all that.

"Why?" Sa'id answered with his own question. He didn't know the man personally but did live in the same dorm and couldn't help but see him and didn't see anything that would lead him to his door. The man did frequent the weed man, tobacco man and was friendly with the sissies.

"Cuz, I like how y'all rock! Y'all be eating together, then doing the thing where y'all be like, Allah something, something," he said and mimicked how Samir made the call to prayer. Sa'id pressed his lips together to keep anything sarcastic from slipping out so he went on. Sometimes you just have to listen and people will tell you where there heart really is. "Y'all get them lil hats, and free world food. And don't nobody mess with the Muslims! Y'all be coming through deep as fuck! Excuse me."

"I see," Sa'id said since it was pretty much what he expected. Dude didn't want to actually practice Islam, which by the way makes one a Muslim. You don't just become Muslim, you practice the way of life and become Muslim by default. He just wanted to be known as a Muslim to reap whatever benefits he could reap. Crazy because the true benefits don't come in this life.

"So, what I gotta do?" He asked eagerly.

"Push my door closed," Sa'id replied. It was slightly cracked from when he entered and the noise of the dorm seeped in.

"Like this?" He asked as he complied from the inside.

"Un-uh, from the other side," he urged. The man shrugged like it was some Muslim ritual and stepped out and pushed it up.

"Like this?" He called into the window. Sa'id just picked his book back up and turned his back. It took a full minute before he caught the hint and moved on.

There were already enough people faking to be Muslim in the ranks and Sa'id wasn't going to be a part of it. Had the man came and asked about the religion he would have taught him, but that wasn't the part he was interested in.

A lot of the Muslims where Muslim in name only and had no idea of what they even claimed to follow. There was safety in numbers so a large number added to that number for safety. Some like Sa'id loved Allah and His messenger more than anyone or anything. It really was Deen or die.

"Fucking guy sucka punched me!" Rabbit declared once he was fully awake. He missed lunch, and yard call getting some well needed rest.

"But..." One of the White Boys was saying until Ghost waved him off. They all saw the taunt and fighter stance Rabbit took before getting knocked out. It was as fair a fight as a fair fight can be.

"Don't worry, they moved him over to C building. Just press the button and he's a dead man," Ghost assured his boss.

"He's already as good as dead. Don't touch him, let him die slow!" Rabbit ordered. What he gleamed from Connor over the weeks was that he had been a raging drug addict. His rich parents enabled him to spend large quantities of drugs. He saw that was his opportunity to punish him for being better than them. Plus get some money in the process.

No, it wasn't Connor's fault for being born into a good family but he was responsible for looking down on everyone else. His white privileged attitude extended to poor whites too. Rabbit endured insult after insult over the weeks while earning his trust. He was one of those 'yahoos' and 'vanilla Isis' Connor often mocked.

He let his guard down yesterday and today got slipped a hefty dose of premium methamphetamine in his coffee.

The flood gates were wide open once more. It took someone to die to get him clean the last time. It may take someone to die this time as well. The Mexicans had finally got a flow of meth but Rabbit was still the man. Controlling the meth market meant he controlled the meth addicts.

Chapter Sixteen

"*Mannnnn*," Malaysia moaned as she pulled up to the club. She vowed never to step foot in the joint again until she owned it but here she was about to step back into the joint. At least it was on her terms and her choice.

"What?" Reecie asked from the passenger seat when she saw her distress.

"Huh? Oh, nothing just thinking about, anyway let's see what lil cuz working with," She said, switching the subject from herself. She offered to drive Reecie to work under the guise of watching her work but had a mission of her own.

Bama had let his guard down since Trouble and Lil-Zay were tucked away in prison. Their ten year sentences gave him a false sense of security that had him hitting the same spots he used to ball out with Trouble. That was bad enough but once he saw Malaysia enter he wanted to take Trouble's girl as well as his freedom.

"Malaysia? Is that you? Damn shawty! You looking good!" Bama cheered but Malaysia already knew that.

"Mmhm," she hummed and lifted her chin above his bullshit. She attempted to walk off but knew he wouldn't let her get away that easy.

"Hole up shawty! I'm buying all dances for the whole night!" He proclaimed and produced a large wad of cash. He used the same network Trouble had established and kept right on getting money.

"Ion dance no more," Malaysia announced with a wave of pride. "I just came to watch my lil cousin dance."

"Shit chill with me then! Sit! Drink with me!" He demanded and raised his hand to summon a waitress.

"Ion know..." She said, playing hard to get. The truth was she had been watching Reecie twerk since she was six. She was here for him.

"Get her whatever she drinking!" He told the waitress and produced a roll of cash that made Malaysia suddenly feel heavy so she sat.

"Brang me a sex on the beach!" She ordered since she heard it on a song. Bama scooted close to her but she shooed him away. "Un-uh! Back up!"

"My bad!" He surrendered and pumped his brakes. He couldn't fuck her in the booth anyway so he slowed his roll. The waitress returned with her drink just before Reecie returned from the dressing room. She was dressed to strip in a halter top and boy shorts.

"Over here sis!" Malaysia called and waved. Reecie didn't hear her over the music but came over when she saw her. Malaysia took the first sip of her drink and grimaced. "Ooh chile!"

"Mmhm," Bama laughed. He knew the fruity drink with the fancy name packed quite a punch. It looked like a lamb but roared like a lion.

"Want me to dance?" Reecie asked hesitantly since Bama didn't ask her last time he was here. He tried to get his dick in her mouth under the table, but no table dance.

"Hell yeah! Just keep dancing right here lil mama," Malaysia instructed. She knew Bama wanted her to stay put and it was going to cost him. A dance cost ten dollars a song and the DJ mixed them in and out halfway through. It was a plan, but not a good one. He was out a few hundred dollars in a few hours but Malaysia was pissy drunk.

"Ion know if she can drive?" Reecie wondered as Malaysia lolled her head as if it weighed too much for her neck. She struggled to hold it upright or even keep her eyes open.

"Don't worry about her. I got her," Bama assured her. He had done this before and knew exactly how to do it.

"You gonna drive me home too?" She asked eagerly.

"Yeah, go get dressed!" He agreed and she rushed off to the dressing room. As soon as she turned he lifted Malaysia to her feet and half carried her to the door.

"Oooooh!" Laquanda sang like a tattletale when she saw Malaysia leaving with the next man. She was going to tattle even if her eyes were closed.

"Awe man!" Reecie moaned when she returned to find the booth empty. Bama had the same reaction when he got Malaysia to his house.

"Awe man!" He said when he tried to scoop her from his passenger seat and realized she had peed on herself. "Still finna fuck your sweet ass!"

Malaysia was too drunk to resist as he carried her up to his door. He had to sit her down to unlock the door, then pulled her inside. All that movement didn't mix with all that alcohol in her belly so something had to give.

"Awe man!" He moaned again when she vomited on his back while he carried her to his room. He was still fussing until he peeled her pissy clothes off and seen her firm frame again. He had seen her naked before in the dim club but she looked even better with the lights on.

Bama went into the connected bathroom and lathered up a rag. He came back to clean the throw up from her face, then washed between her legs. She might have enjoyed it when he dipped between her legs and lapped at her labia, but she was asleep and didn't feel a thing. He didn't let her snores bother him when he slid up and worked the dick inside. It was wet mainly from his saliva but wet is wet, and rape is rape.

"Damn shawty!" He grunted at how tight she was. She certainly couldn't complain about a quick nut or him nutting in her so he did both. "Damn shawty!"

Bama grinded inside her so he could stay hard, then fucked her again. Again, again and a few more times before he wore himself out and finally fell asleep. She was still sleeping when he awoke the next morning.

"Ooooow," Malaysia moaned when her throbbing head nudged her awake. Her vagina throbbed too but that didn't make any sense to her at the moment. Not until she eased her eyes open and didn't recognize the ceiling. It wasn't the one she was used to waking up under.

"Uuuh!" She reeled in a panic when she registered the presence next to her. She rolled off the bed to get away from whoever he was.

Malaysia slowly rose to get a peep at the snoring man in the bed. Seeing Bama confused her even more until she remembered her plan. It didn't include her throbbing vagina so she reached between her legs and felt the telltale crust of dried sex. Guilt wracked her whole being but now wasn't the time to act on it.

She thought fast and quietly rose to her feet and began to look around the room. She had to freeze when Bama moved, but he just flipped over and continued to snore. Malaysia crept around the room and took stock of the money and guns. He had stashes of cash in several draws and pockets but she didn't take a dime. The next room had a table filled with coke, crack, pills and weed. Most was packaged and ready for sale.

Her vagina stopped throbbing when a plan spread a devious smile on her pretty face. She set her plan in motion and unlocked the front door.

"Un-uh!" Malaysia moaned when she found her pissy clothes. There was no time to do anything else so she pulled them on and rushed away from the future crime scene. The rape in progress report sent a flurry of cop cars flooding into the apartment complex.

Malaysia sat on Bama's car in the parking lot. She took the keys so she would have a ride if the cops didn't take it.

The police rushed in with guns high to save the woman from being assaulted. Poor Bama awoke when cops rushed into his bedroom. He was too confused to make sense of what was going on. He didn't register the gun Malaysia put in his hand until the police shouted.

"Gun!" One said and two shot. Bama got hit by both guns but wasn't lucky enough to die. The wounds would heal but the drugs and guns were going to cost him.

Bama was going to D-Block.

Chapter Seventeen

"*I*'m not feeling this at all!" Chuck growled as Lalonda got into his car. He and Shay were usually inseparable but she didn't want to go anywhere near that prison again. Which was fine by him because he had several bones to pick with his sister. A whole damn skeleton.

"You!" She reeled as she fastened her seatbelt. "I let that nigga use my car to go to work with you and daddy! He was supposed to be back so I can go to work tonight."

"Except, he didn't come to work and he ain't here! Where is the nigga is what I want to know," Chuck said calmly this time since he decided to whoop Malcolm's ass. He stayed out of his sister's personal lives as much as he could but, Malcolm was in need of intervention.

"Probably at Sheryl house," she snitched since Malcolm did need his ass whooped. It would either save their marriage or be a going away present.

"Sheryl who? Your friend Sheryl? Why would he be over there?" Chuck asked to make sense of it. He wasn't slow, just had morals and immorality didn't always register immediately. This is why fucked up people have an advantage over good people, because their minds just don't register deceit right away.

"We ain't been friends for a while. And what you think he doing?" She shot back. She saw his jaw tighten when he got it. She also felt the car accelerate a little more.

"You ain't gotta work there you know?" Chuck advised as he drove her there. He stopped short of offering to take care of her but only because he knew she wouldn't accept it.

"Ooh! I can come work with you and daddy! I always wanted to be a damn lumberjack!" She fussed and ended the conversation.

Chuck was thinking more like a secretary since he was pulling that duty himself. He decided to let their daddy talk to her to stay off her bruised ego. Mr. and Mrs. Stanton installed pride in their children and that really can't be undone. Meanwhile he had a mission of his own after he dropped his sister off.

"Sheesh," he moaned at the spot where he witnessed Daryl kill himself. Lalonda looked where he was looking but didn't ask. She had another question on her mind but hated to ask.

"I um," she began and twisted her lips when the words wouldn't come. She needed a ride home in the morning but had trouble asking for it.

"Malcom will be here," he answered for her, looking straight ahead as he came to a stop near the entrance. Lalonda sighed and popped a kiss on his cheek before getting out. She heard the tires chirp when he pulled off aggressively. A slight smirk formed in the corner of her mouth at what she knew was coming.

Chuck rehearsed his spiel all the way over to Sheryl's house. He vacillated between calm, angry, reasoning, and pleading. Malcom had been the perfect husband for years. He treated his wife like a queen and took care of her like a man should. It all went out window when he saw his sister's car sitting in Sheryl's driveway. He pulled in behind it and honked the horn a few times.

"Malcolm! Say Bruh?" He called into the screen door as he knocked on the frame.

"Chuck? What you doing here?" He asked as he came shirtless from the rear.

"Me? What are you doing here? Why didn't you come to work? Why didn't you take your wife to work?" He demanded as Malcolm stepped out the house.

"Oh, I see what going on. Sis sent you to check me? You here to check me, boy?" The liquor said to say so Malcolm said it. A smile spread on Chuck's face when he saw where this was going. Not what he came for but he was with the shits.

"Or we can do it like that!" Chuck cheered and put his dukes up.

"You 'musta forgot how I used to fold yo ass up in gym class?" Malcolm laughed at the distant memory. He didn't remember being a few years older and ten pounds heavier back then. Chuck had been through self defense training at the academy since then as well. He would let Malcolm find that out the hard way.

"Un-uh y'all! Don't do this! Un-uh!" Sheryl pleaded

from the doorway when the men took fighting stances in the front yard.

"Hole on baby. I gotta show this nigga to stay out my business," Malcolm said and threw a looping left hook. It would have done some damage if it connected but it didn't. Instead, Chuck dipped under it and let loose two body shots that dropped Malcolm on the grass.

"Had enough?" Chuck offered so Malcom could quit while he was behind. Malcolm's head nodded since he knew he was whooped but that alcohol helped him to his feet and lifted his fist again. He threw a right this time and got dropped right on the same spot. This time Chuck added an uppercut with the body shots.

"See! I 'tole you to stop, and now you done got yo self knocked out!" Sheryl pleaded to the sleeping man.

"Get the keys to my sister car!" Chuck demanded. Sheryl complied quickly so she didn't get knocked out too. She knew all to well about the Stanton sisters and wanted none of that smoke.

The prison was short staffed so Lalonda was moved from position to position, wherever she was needed. She found herself in the chapel area when church was called. She signed the men in and took a seat in the rear as the chaplain began her show.

"What the what!" Lalonda laughed as Chaplain Jordan remixed Mathew with Motown. She hadn't been to church much since marrying Malcolm but missed the word. That wasn't it but also a proof that you have to be careful who you marry because he will lead you. To the right path or astray, but he's going to lead.

"Now wave your hands from side to side!" the old lady said and the men all said amen. It was another full house since she was passing out her special anointed oil after her show. That's was all Lalonda could bare for one night so she stepped out into the hallway to put some distance between herself and the blasphemy.

'Argh, ughh, igsh, argh,' Lalonda heard from around the corner and went to investigate.

Her eyes went wide at the sight of the source of the noise but it still took her brain several full seconds to process what she was seeing. Her eyes blinked rapidly and brought it into focus. One man was on his knees while another stood over him. Each trust was met with a loud gag from his throat. Not as loud as the screech that escaped Lalonda's mouth.

"Aaaaaaahhhhhh!" She screamed. She screamed and they screamed just as loud.

"What's wrong Miss Jackson?" Stack asked as he and New York came rushing out. They were convicts and let people do what they did but drew the line when it came to the women. Men are by nature the protectors and maintainers of women so that's what they did. Some female officers talked shit and were disrespectful but Lalonda wasn't one of them.

"He! They! Them!" She fussed and pointed since she couldn't find the words. The shock of seeing two men engaged in a sex act had nearly rendered her mute.

"Damn Sherman working I see," Stack said of the sissy

on his knees. He was known for turning cheap tricks for soups and honey buns.

"And Mac-town! I thought you was a Roller?" New York asked louder than necessary to out the gang banger. Both men scrambled to get away while the officer was still stuck. They had the audacity to go right back into the service and sit down.

"He had his, all the way done, he..." Lalonda moaned and wretched like she was about to lose her lunch. "And the other, ugh, argh ugh!"

"Let me get you some water," Stack asked and went to retrieve a bottle of water from the chaplain's office.

"Why would he do that? Why would he let him do that to him?" Lalonda asked as she sat.

"Some niggas can't handle not being with a woman?" New York guessed, then shook his head at his own answer. He had been away from women for the last nine years and hadn't even thought about turning to men.

"Ok, Ok but why would that man, let another man put his thang in his mouth? I'm married and I don't even, well not anymore since my husband wanna..." She was saying until she realized she was saying too much. Especially to a stranger at work.

"Yeah, both are fucked up, but, damn!" New York grimaced at the thought of a man with another man in his mouth. Or hand or anything.

Lalonda had a change of heart towards the gentlemen of D-Block from that moment on. Her soft heart allowed her to believe some of these hard men were victims. The least she could do and would do was ignore them next time she caught them masturbating. That was better than what she just saw. Somethings can't be unseen and in this case unheard. The sound of Sherman gagging on that dick haunted her for a week.

She stepped out of the prison expecting to see her brother but hoping to see her husband. Instead she saw her empty car and didn't know what to think. It wasn't until she reached her empty house that it all came together. Her husband was gone and her marriage was over. She wasn't sure how to feel just yet. After a full shift at the prison she just needed some sleep. Life could wait until later.

Chapter Eighteen

"*H*urry up my nigga!" Trouble heard behind him as he took position in front of the kiosk to order his commissary. It had been victimized so many times by stolen pin numbers it now took facial recognition to log in. He didn't think it was for him so he kept doing what he was doing.

"Slow ass nigga," the voice behind fussed again. He assumed someone else was talking to someone else until a glance behind him showed Gip. The little Roller with the big mouth. He had been shooting at Trouble from day one and now it was about to get him in some trouble.

"Get yo lil homie before I make him look different!" Trouble growled to Rallo.

"He grown," his cousin shrugged and that's as good as a green light.

"Shit shawty if you don't like what I said we can hit the 'boom-boom room'" Gip challenged. The words weren't even all the way out of his mouth before Trouble abandoned the kiosk and headed to the boom-boom room. It was officially a mop closet but being large enough to fight it made it the unofficial octagon.

"Bet not nare 'nother nigga budge!" Stack declared when the Rollers and Riders all started moving over that way.

"Let them handle they biz. Don't draw no heat!" Rallo agreed. Everyone standing around the boom-boom room was a clear indication that something was going on inside the boom-boom room. It was too early for the fuck men to be fucking, so it had to be some fighting.

"Pick up anything and I'ma kill you with it," Trouble informed Gip as they reached the notorious fighting arena. It was filled with mops, brooms and other items that can and have been used as weapons. A 'one' meant strictly hands, balled into fist, thrown as hard as possible. Knees, elbows, feet ands headbutts counted too, just no foreign objects.

"Ion need shit to whoop you!" Gip said loud enough for his homies to hear. Plus he had a plan since Trouble was leading the way. He planned to sneak him as soon as he stepped inside. A valid tactic since they were coming to fight.

"Un-huh!" Trouble laughed when Gip threw a haymaker at his head as soon as he stepped inside the room. He had been expecting it so it was Gip who got caught off guard. He put so much into the punch that he went by when Trouble dipped it.

He came up on the other side and was met with a flurry of punches. He tried to escape the onslaught by ducking but found a knee speeding up towards him. It stood him straight back up and into the line of fire.

More like a firing squad since Trouble squared off and gave him a twenty one gun salute. Gip's head bobbled like a speed bag under the barrage of blows. To make matters worse he got stuck against the wall and couldn't fall. He ended up catching twenty one more shots before Trouble realized he was sleeping.

"I told him to leave you 'lone!" Rallo declared. He did too, but the youngin wanted a rep. He got one too, just not the one he wanted. "That's what he wanted cuz!"

"And that's what he got!" Trouble said, shaking his head. He had been waiting on visit but now needed another shower. He headed to the cell to get fresh for Malaysia and his son.

"You good homie?" One of the Rollers asked as Gip wobbled out of the closet. He wasn't a weeble so his wobble made him fall down.

"Huh? Yeah, he ain't do me nothing!" Gip said. He meant it too but only because he couldn't see himself. He wobbled over to the kiosk and slapped the civilian away in the middle of his video chat. His wife was still screaming when Gip logged him out so he could order his commissary for the next week.

'User not found' the kiosk declared when he took position in front of the camera. He tried again but got the same error message. 'User not found'

"Oh shit!" Rallo howled when he saw what the problem was. "Cuz made you look different! The machine don't recognize you!"

The dorm was roaring with laughter when Trouble made his way through and out for his visit. He was cleaned up, wearing a fresh uniform and smelling like a million bucks. His waves where spinning and new sneakers crisp and clean. He looked like he was getting money in the chain gang.

"Hey baby," Malaysia sang when she saw her man approaching. Her vagina was still sore from the beating it took the night before. That wasn't part of her plan but she still felt guilty and it showed.

"What's the matter?" Trouble asked after his hug and kiss.

"Who?" The guilt made her ask as he took the baby and they took their seats. Trouble squinted at her to see if he could see what she was hiding but it doesn't work like that. "You heard about yo boy?"

"That hoe Bama?" He smiled. His cell phone allowed him to keep his ears to the street so the word of Bama getting arrested had traveled fast. He was about to get hit in the county jail already but Trouble told them to wait until he hit the chain gang, where the knives are bigger. Bama wasn't getting beat up for what he did. He was dying for it.

"What else you heard?" She wondered since someone had to see her leave the club with him. That meant you're fucking even if you wasn't fucking.

"Err thing," he said even though he hadn't heard that yet.

"Let me get you something to eat," she blurted and rushed off to the machines. Trouble missed the guilty look as he looked down at his son. She was back in a flash with all of his favorite machine foods.

"Thanks babe," Trouble said swapping the baby for food.

"You welcome boo," she said and happily watched him scarf down his food. "Slow down! I ain't finna let nobody take yo food!"

"Me neither!" He shot back a little rougher than intended. Prison is a rough place and brings that out of people. Not to mention he had seen enough people get more than enough things taken from them.

The Rollers were getting worse by the day. They would take anything and everything from anyone they could. They even took a guy's state issued uniforms and crocs simply because he didn't have anything else to take. Then beat him up for not having anything else to take. Rallo had no control of his gang in his name. He kept the lion's share of the drug money and forced them to get it how they lived.

"What happened to yo hands? You been fighting!" She asked and answered when she saw his battered knuckles.

"Not really," Trouble said since it wasn't much of a fight. He spanked that baby and put him to bed. Gip was curled up on his rack right now getting a good nap.

"You too much," she laughed but still had a sadness in her eyes. Trouble knew her best and saw it hidden behind the smile and small talk.

"Look, finna make a move later today. Take you a rack and buy yourself something nice. Just you! Not me, not him, not granny, just you!" He insisted, hoping that would make her feel better. It might for a moment but sexual assault doesn't usually heal that quickly.

⁓

"I feel better already!" Malaysia remarked as she walked into Lennox mall. Trouble suggested she go shopping to cheer her up and it was working already.

She used to come here with her girls from the club and spend those dope boys from the clubs money. The baby was with granny so she was free to spend a little dough. Trouble said a rack or so, so that translated to two thousand dollars in her mind. About what she would drop back when she was single so she could make it work.

"Hey miss lady!" A teen beamed and showed off his gold teeth. Young hoes in the hood always went for the gold grimace so he tried it out in the big leagues.

"Yee ain't ready lil man!" She squawked like her old self. She put a wiggle in her walk as she headed to her favorite boutique to cop shit average bitches in the hood wouldn't. Or so she thought.

"Un-uh! Where you been bih!" Laquanda said like she was shocked to see Malaysia in the spot she put her on. The young stripper with her looked between them in awe like they were celebrities. She was doomed with these two as role models.

"Bih don't forget who showed you this place!" Malaysia reminded.

"Yeah, but you ain't been here in a while!" She reminded. Trouble took good care of her when he was home. He even took good care of her now but splurging on bags and shoes wasn't in the new budget. Priority one was stacking back what they lost. Then keep stacking until Trouble comes home so they could invest in and start a legit business.

"Well I'm here now! So I'll show y'all hoes how to

stunt!" She shot right back. Malaysia put on by putting an expensive purse and matching shoes in her basket. Laquanda copped something similar Malaysia she upped the ante and added a scarf.

Laquanda had a good night working the pole and even better late night tricking with a rapper and his entourage. Sure she had sex with quite a few dudes and a woman but they chunked several thousands of dollars her way. Once upon a time it was she who had to watch the superstar Malaysia buy things she couldn't pronounce but now the tables were turned. Or, at least they were supposed to be.

'Whoa!' Malaysia thought to herself when her tally totalled three thousand dollars. She had lost track when she was trying to keep up with Laquanda. The youngin didn't even try to compete since she knew she was out of her league. She would get the knock off versions of all that same stuff for ninety dollars at the West End mall.

"Well I'm finna," Malaysia was sayjng to make her departure but Laquanda wasn't hearing it.

"Un-uh bitch! You ain't finna dip on me again!" Laquanda demanded. "Like you did at the club! I ain't mad cuz Bama do eat ass!"

"Chile I ain't do nothing with that nigga!" She reeled. It was only half true since it wasn't consensual. He actually did eat her ass but she didn't feel it from her drunken stupor.

"Oh, cuz I heard..." She lied to hear what she had to say.

"Brang whatever bitch said whatever they said so I can beat they ass!" Malaysia demanded.

"Don't kill the messenger! You know I got yo back. Next

bitch I hear say some, I'ma whip they ass!" She declared. She would have to whoop her own ass since she started the rumor that was floating around. Bama was a known trick so her leaving with him meant she tricked with him. He had pulled that same trick of getting chicks drunk and taking the pussy. Except he was the only one who got tricked this time.

"I know you got my back girl!" Malaysia cheered. It was good to have a friend since most of her days were spent with her son and talking to Trouble on the phone. She pulled her phone and called granny to keep Trevor for the night. She was going out with her girls.

Malaysia, Laquanda and the young girl called Tootie went out for dinner and drinks before hitting the club. They had to swing by Laquanda's house to shower and change since Malaysia still wasn't letting anyone else know where she lived. Inviting a cousin over cost her a hundred grand and she wouldn't make that mistake again.

"Good thang Ion need no panties in this dress!" Malaysia declared as she stepped out the bathroom. She knew if she went home to shower and change common sense would have talked her into staying put. She could have just enjoyed a rare night of quiet without the baby.

"Gurl!" You killing that shit!" Laquanda cheered as her friend stepped out in the semi sheer dress. Her big, dark nipples pierced the fabric like suckable little daggers. The bottom of the dress stopped just at the bottom of her round ass cheeks.

"Dang!" Tootie sang as she ogled the woman. Her seven dollar tube dress hugged her hips and ass like a mother's love but nothing compared to Malaysia.

"You looking good too lil mama," she told the girl like a pat on the head. They made small talk about trivial hood shit until Laquanda stepped from the bathroom.

"Un-huh bitches!" She announced as she came out looking fierce herself in a flesh colored body suit that made her look naked. Her plump camel toe protruded like it was bare and her breast were just as clearly defined.

"Ok then! We finna look better than the damn dancer at the Chili Pepper!" Malaysia bragged.

"Chili Pepper? Bih we finna hit Club Rosé!" Laquanda corrected. It was the hottest club in the city at the moment in the city known for hot clubs that only last a moment. Malaysia had only heard about it on the radio and was down to check it out.

"Dang!" The young girl repeated since she didn't own many adjectives. The trio smoked a few blunts and drank a few dranks before they headed downtown to the club. Malaysia was DUI as she drove but managed not to get pulled over or wreck the car.

"Come on y'all!" Laquanda directed and led her friends directly around the long line of assorted birds. There were highly embellished chicken heads as well as pigeons waiting to get pregnant by one of the ballers inside. The array of expensive cars pulling up to the valet and dropping rich men off caused a few to ovulate early.

"Y'all on the list?" The burly bouncer barked until he looked down and recognized Laquanda.

"Mmhm," she hummed at him and he undid the velvet

rope to let them pass. "See, yee ain't gotta suck err dick, just the right dicks!"

Poor Tootie nodded and took it is as gospel. Now she had to figure who had the right dicks verses the wrong dick. More than likely she would fall into the adage of kissing many frogs until finding a prince. They were all in awe as they stepped into the swank club. The place smelled just like money from all the money circulation inside.

"We finna hit the VIP!" Laquanda announced and headed in that direction. Malaysia was used to being the leader and felt some kind of way at following. She would claim her position back at the head of the pack as soon as possible.

"Let them in!" Doobie Daddie shouted above his own song booming in the speakers. He was the hottest rapper in the city so the bouncer did what he was told. "Lil mama served the whole crew last night"

"Hey Doobie!" Laquanda sang to the only one who didn't hit. He chucked plenty of bread at her while she danced before leaving her to his entourage.

"Who is this!" Was what he wanted to know when he saw Malaysia. She saw him too with the mouth full of gold, head full of dreds and good looks like his daddy. She was a bad bitch though and bad bitches don't sweat dudes. Especially bad bitches who have a man so she turned her head.

"Un-uh shawty just curved you!" His partner laughed. Doobie laughed too despite the snub.

He still set out drinks as they partied through the night. Laquanda snapped pictures and posted them to social media. Doobie went live and trained the camera on

Malaysia's ass. Literally, since the short dress rose up several times, revealing all that ass underneath.

"Lil mama ain't got on no drawls!" The side kick said.

"Don't need none!" Doobie laughed. He set his sights on Malaysia but she wasn't going anywhere with him or anyone else. He shot his shot, missed and would settle for her number. "Well, at least gimme a number so I can put you in my next video?"

"Mmhm," she hummed skeptically but gave up the digits. She did want to be in a video and she was having fun. She had a ball as her phone buzzed in her purse.

Trouble had called a few times until he saw her tagged on social media by Laquanda. She was having the time of her life while he was just doing time. The sight made him sleepy so he just went to bed.

Chapter Nineteen

"*F*uck it!" Connor proclaimed when he made his decision. No good decision in the history of decisions ever started with, *fuck it*. The worst ideas began with 'fuck it' or, 'all we gotta do is'. This idea was just as bad as any, if not worse.

The wheels had been churning and his desires yearning every since Rabbit slipped him a dose of meth-amphetamine. He assumed the White Boys in the dorm were afraid of him after he beat up their boss. Truth is they wanted to kill him, and were going to kill him when they got the nod. Until then he would just die slow, one day at a time.

"Yeah, fuck it!" He repeated once his mind was made up. He only had a few months left so why not stay high. It would make the time go quicker. Plus he could just quit again once he reached the transition center. At least that's what the devil suggested.

"Look it," JC said as Connor came their way. He was

the lieutenant of the White Boys of the dorm and knew all about him.

"Wish he would give the fucking green light so we can fucking fuck him up!" Kurt fussed. They had to watch the handsome white boy workout and eat good and hated him for not needing them. He fixed his face when Connor arrived.

"Sup guys. I was wondering if I could cop from you guys? I know the Mexicans have some stuff, but..." He said and left off the but. The but was he knew the stuff Rabbit slipped him was A1 quality.

"What happened with you and Rabbit?" JC dared and cocked his head.

"Misunderstanding, no big deal," Connor dismissed with a wave like swatting a gnat. Easy for him to say since he wasn't the one who got knocked out.

"And why you not riding with us?" Kurt demanded and got a sharp glance from JC. "My bad. Never mind."

"No biggie. Hell, I just might! I like how you guys move," he lied. In fact it was quite the opposite. The White Boys moved like a bunch of junkies. Their numbers prevented them from being preyed upon but all they did was get high.

Connor's chin lifted a little as he remembered just how superior he was to them. He just wanted to get high to help him work out longer. Stay up and read, and quit once he got out. No, he was nothing like them.

"Here you go. Give me a hundred," JC said producing a fifty of dope that would have went for twenty on the street.

"That's a hundred? You know what, fine," Connor complained until he caught himself. The dirty white boys needed the money more than he did so he would pay the extra they were charging him. "How you want it?"

"Cash App," he said and passed him the information.

"Need to use the phone? Can't talk business on the blue phone," Kurt explained since he spent a couple hours a day on the monitored prison phone.

"Sure," he agreed and accepted the call. The two White Boys looked at each other as he dialed his family's number into the phone. He fell into the trap just like Rabbit said he would. He became more vulnerable by the day, every day he used the dangerous drugs. Little did he know he was paying for his own hit. A group of Bandos waited for the word to take what he couldn't get back.

"What you got left? Bankhead want an ounce," Stack asked while on the phone.

"Just an ounce," Trouble insisted. He had several ounces left but decided to split it among his Riders. He made sure his whole team was eating to keep them off the fuck shit. Rallo was a selfish motherfucker who only looked out for himself. He had a few lieutenants helping move product but he was the only one really eating.

Precisely why the Rollers were on the fuck shit. They were like bands of Vikings on an English country side. They preyed on civilians or even each other to avoid a war. There was always a reason to violate one of their own and someone was sure to get their ass whipped everyday.

"He want it. I'll take it to him at church call," he offered making Trouble tilt his head and purse his lips dubiously.

"Mmhm, thought you was just coaching?" Trouble asked since him delivering it was a service and services get paid for.

"Yeah, I got something I need to handle. Ion need my girl all in my business," Stack said on the surface with a smirk else underneath. He was going to add a little tax to the price of the ounce to handle that business. He scribbled the Cash App to send his cut to and handed it to Trouble.

"$PBTPTessy?" He asked and wondered where he heard that name from. The names Bessie, Tessie, Jessie, and Nessy had been circulating on the low for weeks.

"Shawty, you ain't heard about pussy by the pound?" Stack asked like he couldn't believe it.

"You mean, beats by the pound? Mannie Fresh ndem? My granny used to love them!" Trouble cheered. He was about to go into a few Hot Boy classics until Stack spoke up.

"Naw nigga, pussy. Pussy by the pound! Bessie, Tessie, Jessie and Nessy. Them big bitches who work in the kitchen. They fucking and sucking like crazy!" He cheered like they just pulled into Six Flags. Fair since a good blow job is better than a rollercoaster.

"Sho nuff?" Trouble asked and squinted as if some ancient mystery was being explained. It sure explained why everyone was trying to work in the kitchen all of a sudden. His mind shifted to Malaysia's distinct attitude as a late. He had wondered if there was some new dick in her life. He was still wondering long after Stack had gone with the ounce.

"Fuck it," he thought and set up an appointment for

himself. He saw Stack used the code for Tessy so he went with Jessie.

After making his moves he made his move over to the kitchen. He passed by a man looking very relaxed and knew he was in the right place. Luckily there wasn't a line as usual because he wouldn't wait in a line of men for the same woman. Like dudes in the dorm waiting to be served by one of the sissies.

Each dorm had a few punks turning tricks for treats. A lot of men think getting head from a guy isn't gay but it is. Some dudes masturbated daily, weekly or as needed while others just exercised self control and didn't let their desires get the best of them.

Then some others had a Fee-fee. The chain gang contraption was made in a variety of ways but all served the same purpose, to bust a nut. To clear the pipes, get straight, release the pressure or whatever. The Fee-fee could handle it. It usually consisted of a latex glove wrapped in socks, toilet tissue holder for smaller dicks or soda bottles for the truly ruined.

It can be lubed with baby oil, anointed oil, or even hair grease. A hot wash rag can add heat and one guy even hooked up batteries to his for vibration. Some people shared them since the glove can be swapped but that's still weird as fuck. Just not as weird as the guy who made a whole dummy out of mattresses with a disposable pocket for the Fee-fee. He rented it by the hour, night or weekends. The warden found it during inspection, but let them keep it. It was a lot less paperwork than a rape charge.

Those who knew about pussy by the pound bought pussy by the pound or throat by the ounce.

"You Trouble?" The large light skinned kitchen steward asked when Trouble arrived.

"Uh, yeah," he said nervously, then cleared his throat confidently. "Yeah, that's me."

"You tryna fuck?" She asked hopefully since she liked the look of him. It still amazed her that handsome men paid to have sex with her. She would ogle them from below as they fucked her throat from above.

"Not this time. I'll just take some head," he sighed. Everyone knows big girls got the best pussy but he took a pass out of loyalty for his lady. There was a good excuse for Malaysia showing her ass in the club so he would let it slide.

"Awe, Ok then," she sighed as if she missed out. She wore knee pads under her pants so she sank to the floor of the office. Trouble was rock hard from the anticipation by the time his wrestled his dick free from his uniform pants. She wrapped it in a rubber and went to work.

"Damn it man!" Trouble shrieked when she swallowed his whole dick whole. A suck, tongue swirl and another suck and he was done. "Fuck!"

"The pussy even better!" Jessie bragged after finishing him off in seconds.

"Next time," he gasped between gulps of air. His knees buckled as he tried to put the dick away.

"Promise?" She pleaded and Trouble saw an opportunity.

"Tell you what, give me your number..." He proposed and she twisted her lips in thought.

"Warden Davis said we not 'sposed to" Jessie asked so he could talk her into it. His head nodded upon hearing they were working for the same pimp. Trouble wasn't a hoe though and had plans of his own.

"Warden Davis ain't down here sucking these dicks tho is she? You wanna make some real money? Or naw?" He asked and began to turn away.

"Hell yeah!" Jessie cheered. She liked all the dick she was getting but liked the money even more. That got her number into Trouble's pocket and away he went.

"What's up Jone?" Stack asked as they passed by. He was going into the store room Tessie worked out of while he came out of Jessie's area.

"Worth err penny!" Trouble declared. Especially since he figured how to make it pay for itself.

Malaysia got some get back but being raped a second time in her short life broke something inside. The night on the town was just what she needed to get back to feeling like herself. She had a hangover from overindulging but had a cure for that.

"Mmhm, don't mind if I do!" She told the blunt clip in the ashtray. There was still some wine in her glass so she sipped from that as well. She had just settled in to get buzzed when her phone buzzed. She wanted to ignore it until she saw it was Trouble. Her ass would be in trouble if she ignored him again like she did last night in the club.

"Malaysia?" Trouble groaned, feeling slightly guilty about getting his dick sucked.

"Hey baby!" Malaysia cheered. She genuinely missed him from missing his calls last night.

"You still coming today?" He asked when he didn't hear any road noise. She would usually be on the highway by now so they could spend every possible second together.

"Mmhm, walking out the door right now!" She said. It wasn't technically a lie since she rolled out of bed at that instant to make it true. "Let me go so I can make moves."

"Ok then. See y'all when you get here," he said to do some hustling of his own. He needed to run the check up to make a hefty investment in his own future.

"Ain't no y'all today!" She fussed at the thought of going the opposite direction to pick up their son. Instead she called granny and let her know she wouldn't be there until this afternoon.

"Mmhm!" Granny hummed as in, 'don't start that shit'. Many of the children she got stuck with raising started off just like that. Including Malaysia's mother.

"For real Granny! Me and Trouble need some time alone!" She stressed. It made sense to the woman who agreed just as Malaysia's phone buzzed again. She switched over and took the call from Laquanda.

"Bitch! You missed all the fun!" She squealed.

"I'm sure I did," Malaysia hummed since she knew they had different interpretations of fun. They both had fun at the club but Laquanda had sex with a couple of the rapper's entourage and that was fun for her too. She wasn't sure why but she heard herself ask, "You fucked Doobie Daddie?"

"Nuh-uh, but I think Tootie sucked his dick. She always got some nigga shit in her mouth," Laquanda laughed as if she didn't. "Anyway, you hanging out with us tonight?"

"Naw, I got a baby, remember," she reminded even though she was the one acting like she didn't.

"Chile you got a granny too! Shoot ole girl a few dollars. Tonight finna be lit!" She proclaimed. "Doobie want us to come to a pool party at his house!"

"I'll see girl," she said as Trouble hit the phone. She said her goodbye and talked to him the rest of the way down.

"Ok then," the guard nodded when Malaysia arrived cute and in conformance to the dress code. She was fifty/fifty on conforming and had to hit the dollar store on more than one occasion. The rules were the same, just different officers didn't mind.

"I ain't playing with y'all today!" She laughed as she was processed in. Her ID was ran for wants and warrants as she went through the metal detector. No alarms went off on either so she was cleared to go in. Trouble wasn't far behind this week since he didn't have to beat anyone up.

"Hey baby! Where the baby?" He greeted and frowned when he saw she was empty handed.

"With granny 'ndem. I needed a break," she said and put her tongue in his mouth.

"Hmp," he grunted anyway since he saw her break on her social media. He followed Doobie Daddie's page too and knew she wasn't at the after party with Laquanda and Tootie. That prevented him from asking questions.

"Hungry? I know you is," she said and rushed off to get what she could out the machine. Being an hour late cost him some of his favorites but she got the others. Plus put a little extra in her walk for him to look at.

"Appreciate it," he said and dove into the food. She filled him in on the latest from the hood while he ate. Nothing he didn't know since his cell phone kept his ear to the street. He still ran the Riders from the joint even though Pablo was the face in his place.

"Did you get yourself something?" He asked as he polished off the burger and moved on to the chicken sandwich.

"Um," she paused since she spent double what he offered. That's not what he asked so she answered, "I did! Thank you daddy!"

"You gonna get me in trouble," he laughed when she leaned over the table and stole a kiss. The officer saw it but didn't trip it. Some had something to say if a daddy played patty cake with his daughter. Some would open the side room for a few minutes and let you get right for the right price. Trouble hadn't found that out just yet.

"Your name is Trouble!" She reminded and lit up the room with her magical laughter. It made Trouble know everything was going to be alright.

"Look, I'm working on a move. If the shit go through we finna make double or triple what we making now!" He advised. He left out that it came with a blow job but she didn't need to know all that.

"We? You French?" She shot back.

"We as in us nigga. We a team. Fiddy/fiddy!" He assured her.

"Ok then!" She shot back since she was now justified in what she spent. It was nowhere near half and she saw some bad ass boots she just had to have. She could get them now since it was half her money.

"I'ma need you to get with Pablo 'ndem soon," he said. Once he got it in order he would start moving his own packs into the prison. Even if he had to fuck big Jessie to get it.

Chapter Twenty

*S*obriety can bring out the worst in some people. Mainly junkies who become irate and combative when they can't get high. Everything is wrong with the world until they get a hit, pull, snort, pill or swallow.

The same holds true for those looking to escape some pain or problem. They could and would hide behind some drug or alcohol, hoping the problem would go away. The problems don't though, and will be waiting right there when they come down. Drugs and or alcohol are never the solution because only in the remembrance of Allah do hearts find rest.

Malaysia was of the second type of junkie. She didn't drink and smoke for the sake of getting high but to ease the bad memorizes. The bad taste of growing up poor, in a bad side of town with a bad boy for a boyfriend. She was cool with the good side but this was the bad side.

"Fuck these folks," she decided and lit a blunt as she rode. It wasn't smoking and driving once she put the Telsa on autopilot. She would have a hard time explaining that to the police if she got pulled over but luckily she didn't. She had a good buzz going by the time she reached her granny's house.

"I'm finna be like Malaysia!" One of the remaining girls declared as she began to dance in the front yard.

"Nuh-uh! I'ma be her!" Another announced and joined her. Neither wanted to be like Reecie even though she was a dancer too.

"I'ma be like hammering Hank Arron!" Granny declared as she came out swinging the broom. Cars has slowed or stopped to watch the prepubescent girls shake what hadn't fully developed yet. Especially their minds which made them look up to the fucked up role models around them.

"Un-uh granny!" The girls pleaded as the elder woman chased them around the yard. Malaysia pulled up in the middle of the whooping.

"What y'all did now!" She fussed and giggled as she came upon the whooping.

"These lil heifers wanna be damn strippers! Got a black woman in the white house, but they wanna shake they lil asses!"

"Shake they lil backs you mean! Ain't nare one of them got no ass!" Malaysia laughed. Loud enough to make her granny squint at her. It was funny but not that funny. This chick was high.

"Mmhm. How my grandson?" She said since she knew she had just from visiting Trouble.

"Fine!" She said meaning fine as hell. The pushups and pull ups had him looking right.

"Y'all ain't been in none of them side rooms have y'all?" Granny asked and tilted her head.

"I wish!" She reeled because she wanted some sex. Consensual sex, while she was wide awake. "I got invited to Doobie Daddie's pool party!"

"They let babies come?" Granny asked since she didn't intend on babysitting again tonight.

"Ion think so but I wasn't asking you to watch him," Malaysia huffed with attitude.

"Mmhm," the old lady shot back. "Shoot, you need to let these lil heifers 'spin-a-night with you so I can get my groove on!"

"At the american legion dranking gin with them nasty ole men!" Malaysia laughed.

"Mmhm and them nasty ole men pop a Viagra with that gin and..." She was saying, but saying to someone who would rather not hear the details of old people fucking.

"You know what!" Malaysia cut in before she described how the older men beat up the box. "Tell them girls to pack a bag. They are finna 'spin-a-night!"

"That's so sweet of you chile!" Granny declared. It really wasn't since Malaysia just needed a babysitter. She was going to a pool party.

"If this phone say Malaysia what you do?" Malaysia asked as she wrapped up her briefing.

"Don't answer it!" The older of the two answered incorrectly. Malaysia shook her head and turned to the younger one.

"If it say Malaysia we do answer it!" She answered correctly.

"And if it say anything else?" She asked hopefully.

"We don't answer it!" The girl cheered.

"That's right! Now, Trevor sleep. Don't wake him up. Don't go in my room, stay out my clothes, don't eat my..." Malaysia warned. It was a waste since the girls had already decided on what they wanted to do the second she left them alone. There was a fridge full of food with no lock on it like at home. Fuck those clothes and her room and the other things she was worried about. They were going to get full.

"Ok!" They sang together. Malaysia knew that song but left anyway. Her timeline was buzzing about Doobie Daddie's pool party all day. She couldn't wait to go live from the jacuzzi.

"Where you at bih!" Laquanda fussed when she took her call.

"Speeding towards your house!" She said as she did just that on the highway. The radar detector detector a radar and slowed the car through autopilot. She managed not to pull on the blunt she was smoking until she passed by the highway patrol car.

Malaysia was good and high by the time she reached the hood. The exotic car turned heads as she pulled into Laquanda's apartment complex. The goons remembered the face and didn't jack her for the car. It could still get stolen if parked over night but no one was going to put a gun in her face and take it.

"Bout dang time!" Laquanda fussed as she came down her steps with Tootie in tow. Both put on a good show with their bikini tops and sarongs wrapped around their waist.

Malaysia wore a similar setup except her sarong was sheer and her bottoms were a thong. The high heels ensured her the attention she desired.

"Anyway! Let's go stunt on these hoes!" Malaysia declared as they climbed in.

The car did most of the driving once again as they rode out to the Atlanta suburb of Stockbridge. Houses pack more punch per dollar out there so the million Doobie dropped on his gave him plenty of house. The backyard looked more like a hotel with the pools, jacuzzis and patios. The party was in full effect when they got there.

"Dang!" Tootie exclaimed when she saw the millions of dollars worth of cars pulled in the driveway, on the grass and side of the road.

"I'm prolly finna get pregnant tonight," Laquanda nodded to herself. With all these ballers she was definitely fucking one of them.

"You stupid!" Malaysia laughed assuming she was playing. She wasn't though since a baller baby daddy was her ticket out those raggedy apartments. Malaysia shook her head as if that's not what she had done. She didn't necessarily try to get pregnant but didn't try not to either.

"Me too!" Tootie decided since she didn't know any better.

The banal banter came to a screeching halt when they arrived around back. The area was packed with beautiful women and handsome men. Come to find out they got stunted on instead of doing the stunting since they looked regular compared to the exotic beauties running around. Except Malaysia who held her own with most of them.

"Un-uh!" Malaysia laughed as a topless woman ran by

being chased by a young man dripped in platinum and diamonds. She opened her mouth to say how she would never go out like that but Laquanda had already pulled her top off.

"Hey!" Laquanda sang and took off running after the guy. Tootie looked to Malaysia to see what she should do. Malaysia shook her head so she kept her top on.

"Let's get us a drank!" Malaysia decided even though she really didn't need one. She was pretty tipsy already but knew what awaited when she became sober. She had no intentions on dealing with those demons any time soon and headed to the bar.

"Malaysia?" A man called when they finally received their drinks. Along with the stern looks from the bartender they didn't tip. The drinks were free but it was customary to tip.

"Oh hey Pablo!" She cheered when she saw Trouble's right hand man. Lil-Zay was his sidekick but Pablo ran the show after he went down.

"Trouble said you was supposed to get with me soon?" He asked and tipped the lady on her behalf.

"Yeah soon, but Doobie invited us," she explained.

"Oh cool. He inside. Come on," he said and led the way inside. Malaysia was glad Tootie followed her as she followed him inside. Tootie held her breath as she walked into the mini mansion.

"Yo bruh! Here go Trouble's girl!" Pablo announced as they made it to the den. Doobie and company were posted up on a huge leather sectional in front of a hundred inch TV.

"Hey it's miss 'likes'!" Doobie laughed with weed smoke billowing from his mouth, nostrils and ears.

"Huh?" Malaysia asked and put her hand on her hip. The move drew even more attention to her curves as the rapper explained.

"That pic I posted of you from the club got more 'likes' than my new car!" He said and turned his phone.

"Oh, Ok then," she said and downplayed her excitement. Her whole timeline didn't have as many likes in a month.

"Let's see if we can top that!" Doobie said and pointed his phone. His latest album was already playing so her hips started rolling. The rapper was flanked by two bad chicks but she had his full attention.

Malaysia enjoyed the attention and swayed her hips along to the bass line. Tootie hadn't refined hers quite yet and twerked like she was still in the club. Doobie had seen enough and pulled Tootie aside to feel her up. Once the song ended she joined the drinking, smoking and partying. The video had tens of thousands of views from all over the country. Including the gentlemen of D-Block.

"Excuse me? Where's the bathroom?" Malaysia finally asked. She didn't want to leave the party but didn't want to pee on herself either. A woman pointed so she rushed off in that direction. The first door was a closet, then a pantry and then a bathroom but Laquanda was bent over the toilet getting dug out.

"Shit!" She whined and set out in search of another bathroom. She couldn't find one but did see a large potted plant. It would have to do. She squatted over and pulled the thin strip of fabric separating her from being naked and let it rip. She almost made it too.

"Really?" Doobie asked as he came around the corner with a bottle in one hand and Tootie in the other.

"I..." She was saying as he passed but kept on peeing. There wasn't much to say since he had peed in that plant before himself.

Malaysia was nosey enough to follow the direction she saw him take Tootie. She went up the steps and peered into a cracked bedroom door. She could only identity Tootie by her shoes in the air. They may have been from Payless but paid off. Doobie was between her legs bouncing up and down in her box like kids in a bouncy house. At least there was an empty condom wrapper on the floor. Either way, it killed her crush on the rapper.

Chapter Twenty-One

"*My* nigga!" Pablo cheered when he took the call from the chain gang.

"Sup shawty. She good?" Trouble asked. He planned to beat around the bush for a few before asking about Malaysia but it blurted out before he could stop. The heart does shit without checking with the head first.

He had seen the videos from the pool party the whole city was talking about. Including Malaysia shaking her fat ass for rich niggas with big jewelry. There was already a clip of Laquanda getting back shots in a bathroom circulating at the speed of the internet.

"Hell yeah! She can't drink for shit! They were turned up tho!" He replied. Malaysia wouldn't remember but she put on real good after she got real good and drunk.

"She ain't..." Trouble began but couldn't finish. That's the thing about being hard, you have to keep that same energy at all times. "Just look out for my people."

"Say less bruh! I got you and that's on Ridell!" Pablo

swore, not knowing he just swore by a snitch. He had kept an eye on the drunken girl all night, then kept the wolves away by taking her to his house after the party.

"Anyway, that's not what I called 'fo," Trouble said and switched to business. "I may have a mule down here. I need some ice! That shit is a gold mine in this joint!"

"Meth? Shit, a'ight. I'll hit up them white boys up in Cherokee county," Pablo agreed.

"Cool. I'm still working on big girl. May have to take one for the team and fuck her big ass," he laughed and broke down PBTP.

"Do what you gotta do my Rider! I'll find out what the biz is on this side," he assured him.

"Cool. I'll have Malaysia bring you the bread when its time," Trouble said. They kicked the shit for a while to fill him in on what was happening in the streets.

"Oh no!" Malaysia whined when she awoke under another unfamiliar ceiling. She instinctively reached between her legs to see if she had sex without her knowledge once again. She was relieved to find her bikini bottom in place and was no more sore than she had been.

"Uh-oh! The party animal is awake!" Pablo laughed from the doorway. He was wearing different clothes indicating that it was a different day.

"Where..." She began to ask but didn't like how that sounded. "Are my girls?"

"Um, the one you came in the house with stayed there. The other chick left with some dude," he explained but didn't know their names. It took Malaysia a moment to put his explanation together.

"What!" She reeled. Laquanda leaving with a dude wasn't a shock but Tootie staying behind with Doobie Daddie came as a shock. Her face began to twist until she remembered she didn't have a crush on him anymore. A more pressing thought came to mind at the moment. "Did you fuck me?"

"Uh no," Pablo laughed like 'duh!'. Then got indignant about the question. I know these niggas out her do some slime shit, but Ion rock like that! Trouble is the boss, plus he my nigga! That's why I carried your heavy ass up all them stairs!"

Some men begged him to leave her behind so she could be sexually assaulted once again. Pablo wouldn't leave his worst enemy in that position so he definitely wouldn't leave his partner's girl in that position. He was a couple of years older than Trouble but had great respect at how he moved.

That doesn't mean he didn't check out her ass when he put her in the bed. All that ass hanging out the thong has his dick harder than GED social studies. To make matters worse, her legs came open when she flipped over. That thin strip of cloth couldn't hold the fat vagina behind it. He pulled a comforter over her and went to bed.

"I am getting a lil chunky," she laughed. She was suddenly uncomfortable in the skimpy outfit even though his eyes never left her face. Malaysia always kept clothes in her car, which brought her to her next question. "Where my car?"

"I pulled it into Doobie's garage. Your phone in there

too. I'll take you to it," he offered and stepped out so she could get up.

Malaysia hit the connected bathroom to relieve her bladder before stepping out into the hallway. She saw the stairs and descended to the main floor.

"Dang!" She said of the nice house. Pablo had good taste and tastefully decorated his home.

"What's wrong?" Pablo asked as he came from the kitchen with food in hand.

"Huh?" She asked instead of repeating herself. Her stomach growled loudly and stole the show. Luckily he had that covered too.

"Here you. McDonalds not fucking with me!" He bragged as he passed her his version of an Egg Mcmuffin. She bit into it and nodded her thanks.

Malaysia crossed her arms over her chest as they rode back to Doobie's house for her car. His house was in the next suburban town and she stared off into the serene surroundings. She felt even more naked without her phone. It was nearly noon and she knew Trouble should have called by now.

"We here," Pablo said but she realized he was on his phone when she turned. A moment later they pulled onto Doobie's block, then into his driveway.

The call got one of the hangers on who hung around the rapper to open the door. Doobie was already up and active after the late night party. He and Pablo embraced and stepped aside to talk. Meanwhile, someone wanted to talk to Malaysia.

"Girrrrrrllllll!" Tootie sang as she wobbled out of the den.

"You was with Doobie all night?" Malaysia asked and squinted at her to see what she missed that a famous rapper did see. Now that she wasn't looking down at her she noticed just how pretty she was. Her near yellow skin was near flawless and her features perfect. Thick lips, high cheekbones and chinky eyes.

"Yup! And we did it all night long!" She giggled and gushed like a schoolgirl.

"Dang!" Malaysia moaned at missing out. Having a man is a good reason to miss out but he was gone so she didn't have a man at the moment. She was stuck at home with a baby while all her friends were having fun. "Anyway, I'm finna go. You need a ride?"

"She good, I need her to hang out with me today!" Doobie declared as he returned before Tootie could answer.

"Ion even got no clothes!" She whined with a giggle.

"Then I'll take you shopping," he shrugged since money ain't a thang.

Malaysia was nearly in tears as she drove back towards the city. Her friends were living their best lives and she was just living. All she had to look forward to was picking up her son and sitting at home.

"I'm finna go shop!" She told herself. Trouble said they were fifty/fifty, so she could spend more money if she wanted to. And wouldn't even have to say anything since it was partly her money. Besides, Tootie was about to go shopping. Her phone buzzed halfway through her justifications.

"Bih, why Tootie laid up with Doobie Daddie!" Laquanda fussed jealously.

"I know right," she whined and pouted. "Anyway, I'm finna go shop!"

"Pick me up!" Laquanda demanded. Malaysia was closer to her apartment than to her granny's house she detoured and headed that way.

Surprisingly Trouble hadn't blown her phone up all night so she would wait to call him. He had his ear to the streets and knew where she slept anyway. That was another conversation for another time.

"Come in!" Laquanda called out from behind the door when Malaysia knocked.

"What the hell!" Malaysia shrieked when she came in to find the girl hanging upside down on her sofa.

"Girl I struck gold twice last night! I met one nigga with a Jag and another with a Lamborghini! I let both them hit!" She exclaimed but that didn't explain why she was upside down.

"So, why you upside down tho?" Malaysia had to ask.

"Tryna keep that nut inside me! Hopefully one of them niggas knocked me up!" She explained while Malaysia shook her head. "I think they in a singing group or something? They both had on a red vest and bowtie!"

"Oh lawd!" Malaysia laughed at her friend fucking the valet attendants. They flashed the next man's keys and got some free booty. "Well, you cain't ride in the car like that!"

"Hey granny. I'ma be a lil late picking Trevor up. I gotta..." Malaysia was saying but granny cut in with something to say of her own.

"Bitch, your baby ain't even here!" She reminded since

she obviously forgot she had her little cousins babysitting at her apartment.

"Chile I'm just playing with you! We finna go shopping. Need something?" Malaysia said, trying to clean it up.

"Mmhm," granny hummed at the girl slipping. Her company rubbed his Viagra dick on her leg to get her off the phone. "Let me go I..."

"No she didn't hang up on me!" Malaysia laughed after her grandmother did indeed hang up on her.

"Granny tryna get her some pipe!" Laquanda squirmed in the seat.

"Ok now, don't be leaking on the leather!" She laughed, but was serious.

"I got a pad on to keep some of it inside me," the thot happily nodded. They went on with their small talk on the way to spend big dollars.

Shopping did make Malaysia feel better, for the moment. It was like putting a bandaid on a bullet wound. Once again she spent more than she should have but kept a running tally of what it should be. Trouble couldn't check all the accounts himself and had to take her word for it. A double edged sword if ever there was one. Only the people you trust can get close enough to be untrustworthy.

Chapter Twenty-Two

"Just don't say nothing. Court in a few weeks. Don't say nothing...' Sa'id said repeatedly to himself as he approached the Friday prayer. It was held in the same large room that hosted the visitors on Saturday and Sunday.

"As salaamu alaykum Shakur," he greeted an elder brother as he arrived.

"Wa alaykum as salaam," he huffed but his face contradicted the greeted of peace he just offered. Shakur may not always wear his teeth but always managed a smile for his brothers since it's considered a form a charity. The sourpuss look made Sa'id take notice.

"What's wrong?" He asked and braced himself, knowing it could be anything. People joining the ranks of the Muslims for ulterior motives meant lots of unnecessary drama. Both tried their best to keep the ranks pure but it was bigger than them.

"Just look," he said and scanned the room. Sa'id did look and saw the same disturbing images. The number of guest had almost doubled since the week before. Semi discrete hand shakes explained why to the trained eye.

"I know this dude ain't..." Sa'id growled as Jahil made his rounds. He slipped the guest something with each handshake. Prison is a fishbowl and it's hard to keep secrets. Word had circulated that Jahil was slinging dope but this was their holy day. It was also an open call out that inmates from every dorm could attend. The perfect place to distribute dope for dummies.

"Yeah that nigga is!" Shakur growled. The old man would fight but Sa'id reeled him in.

"Patience akhi," he reminded since patience is a form of worship. They turned away and sat on the carpet to silently reflect on the greatness and majesty of their lord until the sermon, known as a khutbah began.

Sa'id and Jahil took turns giving the khutbah even though they were on different pages of the same book. Both used the Qur'an but Jahil gave his own understanding which allowed his to twist it to fit his needs and deeds. He actually had some people believing selling drugs was allowed even though it was totally forbidden.

Sa'id on the other hand followed Orthodox Islam, the same way as their pious predecessors. Islam is not a religion, but a complete way of life. It can't be donned and doffed on Friday and abandoned the rest of the week. He and Shakur shifted uncomfortably on the carpet as Jahil twisted the words of the holy book. He sounded more like a minister from the nation of Islam than an actual Imam. He spoke about politics and current events as if it was a black lives matter rally. Especially uncomfortable to the white, Latin, Asian and others from amongst the brothers.

Both were relieved when the mismatched sermon came to an end. Their relief was short lived when Jahil began to recite the Qur'an as required in the prayer. He mixed and screwed the Arabic like a Houston DJ. After the prayer the brothers mixed and mingled until it was time to return to their dorms. Sa'id tried to ignore the obvious signs of drug slinging and caught up with the brothers he knew to be brothers.

"As salaamu alaykum!" A young brother greeted. He was hard to make out through all the tattoos on his face but Sa'id recalled him from the county jail. The younger stayed on the fuck shit so much he got the name, fuck-shit. He was a Roller and most of them stayed on the fuck shit. He took it to the next level, hence his nickname.

"Fu...I mean," Sa'id began but caught himself.

"They call me Raheem now!" He beamed brightly. The glow of belief lit his eyes brightly.

"Raheem! That's what's up!" Sa'id cheered and shook his hand. "How you make out in court?"

"Sweet! Five, serve one year! I'll be home in a couple months!" He said and realized he forgot something. "In sha Allah!"

"In sha Allah," Sa'id agreed since nothing happens unless Allah wills it to happen. Man can't will unless Allah wills. "Still banging?"

"Huh?" He asked, meaning yes. "I told Rallo I'm finna fall back."

"Fall back then. Tell him to holla at me if he need to," Sa'id offered. The kid wanted to change his life and Sa'id would help in any way possible. He liked the bad kid for some reason. He was always hyped and animated as if a director just yelled 'action!' They shook, hugged and went their separate ways.

"As sa, um, I'm moozlim now!" The man from Sa'id's dorm said as he came up. Jahil was across the room giving the oath and passing out kufis to any and every one. He wanted to strengthen the community with numbers but that's just like adding plain water to a perfect pitcher of Kool aide. Sure you get more, but its weak and watered down.

"Ya Allah, free me from this place..." Sa'id prayed as he walked away. He used to pray for the guidance to straighten the ranks, now he just wanted out. He would be headed back to court soon, and hoped not to return.

"Yard call!" The various officers called from all around the prison. Most of the gang bangers had mandatory yard calls just in case shit popped off. Trouble had his people come out so he could personally keep his finger on the pulse on his unit. It also allowed him to run a lucrative drug operation on behalf of the wardens. He still had plans but had yet to put them in motion.

"Sup y'all! Err body good?" Trouble asked with the diplomacy of a diplomat. It was part of the appeal that had people swearing oaths on his name.

"Err thang good!" Was the consensus of his people. A few had a few issues here and there but all managed to get worked out peacefully. The whole crew was eating good, now they had to maintain it. The Rollers on the other hand were in chaos.

"Look, that fuck-boy George just got out the hole!" Rallo growled of the Roller who got caught fucking in the chapel. The Rider he was wapping out with got ejected from the gang without a drop of blood being shed. He simply joined the Bandos where he belonged. George was getting off so easy.

"He need to feel it!" Mac Town huffed. He had just been caught down a sissie's neck at church call too but Stack and New York didn't gossip so it didn't get out.

"I...what the fuck! Is that Fuck Shit?" Rallo was saying until the sight of a Roller in a kufi caught his eye.

"Yeah he took Shahadah in the county. He Muslim now!" One of the young Rollers who knew advised.

"He 'musta got an L?" Rallo asked since a life sentence made many a man a Muslim in name. It's belief in the heart, speech of the tongue and actions of the limbs that make one Muslim in truth.

"Naw, he go home in a minute," the kid shrugged.

"Sho-nuff?" Rallo asked, confused by someone doing something positive.

"Sup y'all. I uh, need to holla at you?" Raheem greeted and asked.

"Ain't shit you can say to me that you can't say in front yo brothers!" Rallo barked. The kid shrugged and went on.

"I'm out. I'm Muslim now," he declared.

"You must have forgot, this shit 'fo life?" Rallo reminded. "Someone call the streets and tell them I said, to wack this nigga mama!"

"Bruh," Mac Town interjected, then whispered in his ear. "If he wanna be Muslim you gotta let him go."

Usually if a gang banger wanted to flip to another gang he had to get jumped out the same way he got jumped in, or put in some work. That didn't apply to men wanting to better themselves through religion. If a man wanted to go to church or the mosque, they would let them. That's how Trouble operated but Rallo was a dick head.

"Shit, may as well let him handle that business before he go," Rallo whispered and nodded towards George who had just stepped out into the sunlight. Mac Town shrugged and fell back before Rallo turned to Raheem. "Take this and go wet that nigga George. Then you free to go."

"And my mama good?" Raheem asked. He had put his young mother through enough already. He wouldn't let her get hurt on his behalf.

"I still might fuck her but ain't no one gonna hurt her," he assured him. Raheem took the knife and transformed back to Fuck Shit one last time. "Hole up shawty!"

"Huh?" Raheem asked when he was stopped in his tracks.

"Take that shit off yo head first! You still a Roller til that shit is done!" He snapped.

"Oh yeah! Ok," he agreed and pulled his kufi off. George had a mouthful of lies to tell about getting caught as he made his way over. He and Fuck Shit met halfway.

George twisted his fingers to give the Roller handshake

but Fuck-Shit had other plans. He was going to stick the man in his arm and be done with this shit for good.

"My bad shawty," Fuck Shit apologized in advance as he upped the banger.

"For what?" George asked just before seeing the blade coming towards him. He lifted his arm to block the blow but didn't. The knife entered his chest, under his arm and popped his heart like a balloon. George dropped dead right on the spot.

"The fuck them niggers got going on?" Ghost said as George dropped to the ground.

'Who cares what those niggers do?" Ghost said as they crossed the yard on their own mission. Plenty people saw the brief violence but the extent wouldn't be known until he was left out on the yard. People get knocked out and sleep through yard call almost every yard call so it wasn't a big deal.

Once it was discovered he was dead, the cops would review the cameras and then it would be a big deal.

"Looks, like, uh! Uh! Uh! You, got, company!" Nutty Bar said as he twerked in front of the bench.

"I see them lil mama," One eyed Dino said. He may have only had one eye but it stayed scanning the yard for danger or prey.

"Fuck them white boys want?" A fellow Bando called Nasty Nate asked.

"Prolly some more of this dick! I used to fuck his face in juvie," Dino bragged just as they arrived. It was true that he did but deflected Nate from knowing where the meth was coming from. Dino spread the weed and tobacco around through his crew so they could eat, but the meth he got from Rabbit went to the medium fortune he amassed over the two decades he spent behind the wall.

"Sup. Have a word?" Rabbit asked when he arrived. He tried his best to ignore Nutty Bar popping and dropping while the other men who liked that sort of thing tossed packs of ramen noodles.

"Sure," Dino said and stepped aside. The people who vote on the Oscars should have seen this scene of mortal enemies acting as if they weren't going to kill each other, first chance they got. Both took from the other what can't be gotten back. An eye, and a virginity.

"I got that bread for you," Dino said as part of his plan. To keep being punctual until he was given a large enough pack to run off with. He would just keep the money and dare the White Boys to do something about it. Sure they had numbers but he had raped a good number of them through the years.

"How would you like to keep it?" Rabbit offered and waited for him to agree like he knew he would.

"Who is it?" Dino wanted to know since he knew the offer had strings attached.

"An uppity white boy name Connor!" He snarled.

"Oh yeah! Pretty, blonde hair thang! Got all them muscles and..." Dino was saying and squeezed his dick.

"Yeah, him. I want you to see about him," Rabbit asked.

"I'll fuck him for what I owe, but it'll be double that if

you want him wacked!" Dino explained. He had the upper hand so he could outsource the job and still get paid.

"Just fuck him and I'll still pay double. Keep what you owe me and I'll shoot you the rest when it's done," Rabbit said. He knew most of most of the homosexuals in prison were sick so it would be a perfect going away present. He turned to leave and clenched his ass cheeks as he walked away, knowing Dino was watching. He was, and still holding his dick.

"I'ma fuck you too 'fo it's over with," he told Rabbit's back before returning to his crew. Nutty Bar had twerked up a sweat but was still twerking.

"What was that about?" Nasty Nate asked when he returned.

"You in the dorm with that pretty white boy named Connor right?" He answered with a question of his own.

"Hell yeah! I be jacking on him from the shower when he be working out!" He said, proving they don't call him nasty for nothing.

"Take a couple of gals with you and take the pussy! Its worth a couple racks for y'all to split," Dino said and kept the change.

"Shit, I'd fuck him for free! Consider him fucked!" Nasty Nate cheered. He couldn't wait for yard call to be over so he could do the dirty deed. Again, they don't call him nasty for nothing.

An officer shouted as he came into the dorm.

"What now?" Sa'id groaned even though he didn't mind

being in his cell. It was a lot quieter than the noisy day room. Not to mention be subjected to hearing the oddest conversations. Some young boys were just arguing which rapper had the most money, based on how much they spent on their jewelry.

He gravitated near the TV but the sissies were too close and he didn't need to hear about using empty soda bottles to douche with. Yeah, his cell was safer so he spent most of his day in there reading or writing.

"Someone got stabbed on the yard!" His bunkmate said since he was one of the last to leave yard call. Hundreds of men stepped right over George like he was a puddle. The wound bled internally so no one knew he was dead. No one cared either though.

He was right though and the death wasn't discovered until the next count time. The cameras were reviewed and the brass was called out to investigate.

"Hmp?" Warden Mays hummed and wondered if she could cover it up.

"Ion know ma'am?" Deputy Warden Davis said and thought. The county coroner raised a stink over the last homicide they labeled as a suicide.

"Was he affiliated?" The warden asked and turned to Sergeant Pike for an answer.

"Ummm..." She said and read the hieroglyphs on his face and neck. "A Roller."

"He got locked up from the chapel one night too! Got

caught hung up in another guy," Davis recalled when she read the name off his ID.

"Run the film back. Lock up whoever did it," Mays ordered over her shoulder as she walked off. She wasn't letting these idiots fuck up her bread. The new order of the day was free world charges for violence. That should slow them up enough to get her money up and get up out of there.

Chapter Twenty-Three

"Ewwww! Lil-Zay so dang nasty!" Laquanda fussed and grimaced. That was certainly the pot calling the kettle black since she just fucked two valet attendants raw, in the same night. Luckily for them neither got her pregnant because she was the baby mama from hell, waiting to happen.

"Dropped some 'mo dick in 'yo inbox?" Malaysia asked. They followed him and a few other Riders IG pages to chronicle their time down the road.

"Un-uh! A video fucking some fat gurl! 'Talmbout some pussy by the pound!" She laughed.

"In the chain gang?" Malaysia reeled and came over to see for herself. Sure enough she saw Lil-Zay delivering back shots to a big girl in the cooler. They clicked the hashtag PBTP and saw several men singing their praises.

The PBTP crew also used the hash tag in their own post. The three to four hundred pound women with new hairdos and big girl outfits. New trucks in front of every rib shack and restaurant in the county.

"Girl they be doing thee most!" Laquanda squawked while Malaysia squinted. She strained to recall why those initials rang a bell in her mind.

She was so sure she heard them before she started a mission to find out from where. Laquanda kept on scrolling while she went on a search of her own. A search of her phone lead her to the email she maintained for Trouble. It didn't make sense but she clicked anyway. Her heart skipped a beat when she saw the two hundred dollar payment.

"So..." She moaned to justify it to herself. He was locked up and did need some pussy. "What about me tho?"

"Huh?" Laquanda asked to her moan. She looked up and saw her pouting like she wanted to cry. "Girl what?"

"Huh?" She answered since it was better than the answer. Here she was being faithful and he was fucking. Here she was feeling guilty about fucking up so much shopping and partying while he was spending money fucking. To top it off Tootie was now dating the rapper Doobie Daddie, Laquanda was fucking everyone, while she sat home alone. Laquanda shrugged and went back to her scrolling just as Trouble called. "Hello,"

"Sup shawty, I need you to," he was saying until he caught her tone. "I know baby! I miss you too! I love you!"

"I love you too baby!" She moaned and melted. Those words were just want she needed to hear to soothe her.

"I'ma have Pablo take you out somewhere," he decided for a couple reasons. First because she liked to get fucked up. Second, because she liked to get fucked up so he needed someone to babysit her.

"Ok baby," she sighed since she wanted to get out. She scooped her cousins from their granny house every weekend so she could hang out. Even she had to admit it would be safer than hanging out with Laquanda's ratchet ass. "What did you need me to do?"

"Trying to close the deal on this move. Send five grand to $PBTPJessie..." He said but didn't hear her heart break. She couldn't balk since she had spent that much shopping this week. Now she was about to pay for some pussy by the pound for him.

"Mmhm, Mmhm, Mmhm," she hummed along as she took his instructions.

"You Ok?" Trouble asked but only because he didn't know she knew what a PBTP was. All she was thinking about was something about some ducks. Only because she couldn't say what's good for the goose was good for the gander.

Jessie was a certified head specialist, but didn't fuck much. A few times on the street but only head behind the wall. Something about Trouble made her want him inside of her. He kept pressing the issue of her bringing in the work but she kept pressing the issue of getting him inside of her.

The meth market was booming and he wanted in. Only Rabbit and his White Boys or the Mexicans were really eating. Meanwhile, he had to share the weed, tobacco and phone hustles with everyone including Rabbit and the Mexicans. Pablo was right, he had to take one for the team.

"You a'ight bruh?" trouble asked as he had to practically catch a man as he wobbled out of Jessie's area.

"Yeah, knees, weak. Cain't breath!" He struggled and gasped. Jessie's head was the stuff of legends .It was known to turn legs to rubber so he could relate. He wouldn't mind one of those breathtaking blow jobs right now, but was on a whole 'nother mission.

"The team. You the leader, take one for the team," he coached to himself and tapped on the office door. She called for him to come, so he came in.

"You sent too much! Way too much!" Jessie reeled when he came in.

"Naw, that's plenty. And there's plenty more where that came from! Five racks a week, err week," he said. After reading about business titans like Rupert Murdoch and Warren Buffet he learned how to make an offer that can't be refused. Not refused, but sometimes modified as he quickly found out.

"And that pretty dick! Once a week. Fuck me once a week and I'll do it!" She bargained.

"I'm here for it!" He quickly agreed. Pablo found the connect with a great product and even better price. He had to move on it and now needed a mule to bring it in. He was now face to face with a mule sized vagina. Dudes were back in the dorm fucking other dudes or make believe pussies named Fee-Fee so he wouldn't complain.

"Come get this pussy then!" She dared, leaned back and lifted her large legs. Trouble found himself instantly erect but still let her apply the condom with her lips. He slid between the thick, cellulite thighs and went in.

"Shit!" He grunted and grimaced when he squeezed into the hot, wet, tightness. He was scared to stroke so he wouldn't bust too quick.

"You stupid! It ain't even in!" Jessie laughed and sent ripples through her blubber like a water bed.

Trouble squinted curiously and looked down so he could get the joke he told. He had to shake his head when he realized he had actually slid in between a roll of fat. That's why it was tight, but the wet was sweat.

"My bad," he laughed along with her. This time he watched as he pushed into the fat, slippery lips. It was way better than the crevice he was just in. Too good because two strokes later he nearly died. "Shit! Fuck! Argh!"

"I know right!" Jessie gushed and blushed. She gave her tight box a few squeezes and giggled as he squirmed.

"I need to redeem myself!" He declared and went to work. He really didn't need to redeem anything since she was used to it. He took half a step back and pushed the big legs as wide and high as he could. Then, unleashed the beast.

Jessie wiggled, jiggled, screeched, squished and squashed as he gave that vice like box a thorough beating. A puddle formed under her before flowing onto the floor as she came again and again. Her rolls of blubber shuddered and shook each time she came. Trouble was putting on until the pussy got super good in an instant. Dudes know exactly what that means but will keep on going and wondering if the condom broke. The difference is as abrupt as someone turning the lights on in a pitch black room.

They still keep on stroking until they bust. All those children should be named 'denial'.

"Fuck, you, got some, good..." Trouble was saying but the last words came out his dick along with all the little troubles he skeeted into her vagina.

"And you, sir. Have some wonderful dick!" She replied. "I'm looking forward to next time!"

"Me too! Might not be no week," he heard himself say before he could stop himself from saying it. He cleared his throat and got to business. "My man Pablo gonna come bring you something. Bring it to me!"

"Ok! Un-un-un!" She agreed and gave his dick a few more squeezes. It had deflated some so one of those squeezes pushed it out. That was fine since she had the kind of head that could have made the Twin Towers stand back up. She did, and he went for round three. He was supposed to call Pablo back but it would wait until the morning so Malaysia could get out and have fun.

A new day was dawning and he was coming gunning for Rabbit. Once he got this meth in, it would officially be Rabbit season.

Chapter Twenty-Four

*H*ey officer Stanton!" New York greeted with the crooked smile that made Lalonda feel like a girl lately.

"Clayton," she nodded and stifled a smile. She relished in the attention she hadn't gotten in a while. Malcolm had checked out even before her brother put him out. He hadn't signed the divorce papers yet but stayed gone. She had no choice but to close her heart and clean it out so it would be ready when the next tenant arrived.

"You look nice," he offered awkwardly when he noticed the dabs of makeup she wore that she didn't normally wear.

"Thank you!" She gushed and felt her lonely vagina thump one good time. Malcolm had his most attentive moments missed subtle changes like that. She had once dyed her whole hair a different color for him and Malcolm didn't seem to notice. She smiled a wicked smile before scanning the area. No one was looking so she came out of her pocket. "Here."

"What is this?" New York asked as he accepted the warm offering and tucked it into his pocket. He wouldn't mind a mule to make some money before he went home, but didn't peg her as the type. She was a lonely lady looking for someone to help the twelve hour shift pass.

"Go see!" She said and he scurried off to the mop closet. He was smart enough to not let these hating inmates to see the move.

"Ok then!" She heard him say from inside the closet. She didn't expect to hear anything else once he unwrapped one of mama's famous biscuits. New York pulled the bacon off since he didn't eat pork. He put it in his pocket instead of throwing it away since someone would buy it. The chain gang is weird like that. He quickly scarfed the rest of it down and took a few sips from the faucet to wash it down.

"You might need this," she said as she stuck a soda into the door. Mama's biscuits were big and fluffy but needed something to wash them down.

"Thank you!" He called back and knocked it out. Then fixed up his mop water since he really did do a little work while he was out here pretending to work so they could talk. "That was the best biscuit I, ever had!"

"My mama thanks you!" She smiled on behalf of her mama. Her and her sisters thanked her too because those fluffy biscuits added to their fluffy asses.

"Guess I'll hit the sweet spot!" He laughed and poured a little extra bleach in the bucket. The 'sweet spot' as it was called was a blind spot in the hall where men could look into the booth and masturbate.

"Oh my gosh they went crazy today!" She laughed and shook her head. She used to write them up until she

caught a man gagging on another man. She was still trau-
matized by that so she just ignored the jackers jacking their
dicks. It left globs of baby goo on the floor and wall. One
was particularly backed up and managed to reach the
glass.

"I bet," he remarked and got to work. She stood nearby
but made sure not to look down at the residue left behind.

"So, what, what do you do?" She asked sheepishly.
Mama didn't raise no punks so she cleared her throat and
clarified her question. "When you get horny?"

"Not that!" He laughed as they saw two men pop out
their rigged cell doors and dip into the shower. They had a
good laugh for a second before getting serious again.

"I wouldn't mind if you did," she offered and bit her lip.
She was feeling naughty at the thought of watching him
jack off in front of her.

"I couldn't do that!" He laughed and blushed. Paused,
thought about for a second, then shook his head. "Ion really
rock like that. I be wanting the real deal."

"I get it," Lalonda nodded in agreement. They moved
on to another topic but Lalonda was thinking how, when
and where could she give him the real thing. New York had
some real pussy in his near future.

He wasn't the only one with some unexpected pussy on
the horizon.

"Ion know what you doing all 'dat 'fo" Malaysia told herself
as she shaved her vagina bald in the shower. Something she
didn't usually do. She did usually use the detachable shower

head to get herself before she went out for the night. She bypassed that ritual this evening while ignoring why.

She wrapped up her shower and wrapped in a plush towel to finish dressing. Her hair was laid out thanks to an expensive day at the hairdresser. She was glad Trouble had a new move coming to make up for some of the money she had been spending. She knew exactly what they should have had put up but had no idea how much was actually there. That would require being responsible and she was being everything but.

"A lil head start," she reasoned to her naked reflection as she lit a blunt. She marveled at her young girl fineness in the mirror before getting dressed. Her breast were plump and heavy yet firm and ready. Her stomach was flat and hard and the bikini cut for the c-section wasn't even visible. Below it was a fat, lonely Rabbit.

She tried to ignore the why, when she pulled on the matching thong and bra set. She shrugged it off like no one would see it, but knew someone just might. Why not since Trouble was buying pounds of pussy.

"Shoot!" She pouted and was determined not to cry. She gingerly slid a tiny dress over her head so not to mess up her do, then stepped up into a pair of heels.

"Can we have..." Her little cousins demanded as soon as she stepped from her room.

"Sure! Sure! Go 'head!" She agreed to everything since her mind was elsewhere. Her phone buzzed and her lips twisted at the caller. Still, she took the call. "Hey."

"Hey? That's all I get?" Trouble laughed. She didn't so he continued. "Anyway, give Pablo the rest of that bread. It's going down!"

"I know. You told me. He on his way," she said dryly just as the house phone buzzed as Pablo reached the gate. She quickly pressed the button that raised the gate and granted entry.

"I told him to take you to a movie or something," he said nodding to himself.

"He said that," she said just as dry and Trouble got the hint. Malaysia was attitude prone so he knew to just leave her alone when she got fussy.

"Aight then. I'll see you tomorrow," he said and took for granted that she would take the ride to see him.

"Mmhm," she said and tied him in the race to hang up without saying goodbye.

"The door!" The girls shouted when the doorbell began to chime.

"Yall heifers think Ion hear it!" She snapped. The poor little girls had been called heifers so much they believed they were. "Y'all bet not wake that boy up!"

"Sorry Malaysia," they both whispered as she pulled the door open.

"Sup shawty I..." Pablo was saying but all the titty in his face stole his train of thought.

"Mmhm!" She giggled at the compliment, then handed him the money. "From Trouble."

"Ok. He told you about the movies?" He asked since she was dressed for the club.

"Mmhm. I'm ready," she said and stepped out of the apartment. She turned and gave her cousins a stern look that translated to, 'don't wake that boy up!'.

"I may be under dressed?" Pablo said as he opened the door for Malaysia. That was something Trouble had never done. He even turned his head so not to look between her legs as they opened to sit.

"I really don't want to go to the movies," Malaysia announced once he was seated and pulled away. "Let's go to your spot and chill. Just need some quiet time away from the kids.

"Um? A'ight," he shrugged. He didn't have kids but understood.

"Ugh!" She grunted when a Doobie Daddie song came on the radio. It was hot but reminded her of being alone while everyone else wasn't. "You got kids? A girlfriend?"

"Nope, nope," he said with a proud smirk that made Malaysia wonder.

"Why not?" She needed to know. Dude was handsome, getting money and had a mix of hood and suburban manners that intrigued her.

"Ion know? I guess, it's too important," he guessed.

"What, a girlfriend?" She reeled and grimaced. She knew people who went together for a week or even just for the night. What was so important about that, she needed to know as well.

"Yeah. My time. My life, me. I'm important. I want a chick who is down to build a life," he reasoned. Malaysia tuned him out after that so she wouldn't leave a puddle on the leather seats. His ambition turned her on like never before. "Loyalty is everything."

"Tell me about it. I'm being a faithful to a nigga in jail who buying pussy in jail!" She fumed. Pablo knew but didn't know she knew. He knew now, but didn't know what to do next. The rest of the ride was made in silence as they contemplated the future. Not tomorrow, of next month, but the rest of the night.

"Well, here we are," he announced as he opened the door and stepped aside.

"Where is your room?" She asked as she stepped inside. She looked up the steps towards the guest room she slept in.

"Last room on the..." He was saying but she was already heading up the steps. He shook his head and followed behind her.

Malaysia made the most of her brief head start and pulled the dress back over her head. She wasn't as concerned about the hairdo this time.

"Man..." Pablo sighed as he came in and found her on the middle of his bed wearing nothing but the heels. He was a loyal dude but dude wasn't loyal to his woman.

'You really doing Trouble a favor. Them other niggas gonna fuck her, turn her out, pass her around' the devil whispered. His work was done once his head began to nod. The devil is a liar but he was right about that. Malaysia was scorned and liked to get fucked up. The perfect storm to end up on some home-made porn site getting passed around.

"You do know what to do don't you?" Malaysia asked when she leaned up and found him stuck.

"Huh? Oh, yeah," he said and pulled his shirt off while kicking his shoes off. He kissed her ankle and skipped the rest of the leg and went straight for that bald pussy. Something else Trouble never took the trouble to do.

"Dang boy!" She moaned as his tongue found its mark. He lifted her legs high by her heels and lapped at her labia like the depended upon it. "Dang boy, dang boy, ooooh dang boy!"

Malaysia danged until her body silvered and shook. Pablo could only get his pants to his knees because he urgently needed to get inside of her. He reached over and grabbed a condom from bowl of condoms on the night stand. She greedily licked her own juice from his lips, tongue and chin as he slipped inside of her.

"Dang boy!" She grunted when he slammed to the bottom of her box.

"Damn girl!" He replied equally amazed at how tight she was. Malaysia knew she had some super good pussy so she raked her nails across his back. The painful pleasure was usually enough to distract Trouble from coming too quickly. It didn't work with Pablo. He came with a loud grunt, but kept right on fucking her.

Malaysia made a decision before he reached the second of what would be many nuts. Trouble was too much trouble, she chose Pablo.

$\mathcal{M}$uhfucka is pretty!" Gator said and licked his lips as Connor worked out below. He had been wanting to fuck the pretty white boy. Now he could get paid to do it.

"Hell yeah!" Nasty Nate agreed. He always insisted on going first when they ran trains, even though he was sick as a dog. He would leave a nice puddle of infection in a rectum for the next men in line for that behind.

There were four Bandos in the dorm but four more came when word got out about some fresh meat. They were tired of fucking the same old chain gang hens and were down for a good old fashion rape. Plus Nasty Nate saw how hard the hard bodied white boy worked out. Especially lately since he was hyped up on the meth. They watched and waited he stayed high and stayed awake for a week. When he finally crashed they came crashing in.

"The fuck?" Connor asked calmly to the sudden intrusion. He was shirtless and sweaty from his workout, which turned the booty bandits on even more.

"You know what the fuck going on shawty!" Nate growled and bared his teeth and dick. "Shit on the dick or blood on the blade! However you want it?"

"Oh, so you guys came to fuck huh?" Connor nodded for clarity.

"And some head, pretty white boy!" Nate said as his dick throbbed to life in anticipation.

"Finna run a train on you!" One of the other Bandos proclaimed. "Rabbit sold you to us white boy!"

"Did he now? Ok, well lets get those pants off fellas!" Connor cheered and rubbed his hands together greedily. Eight men with knives stood between him and the door. They had the numbers but odds still weren't in their favor. The odds went down even more along with their pants. How the fuck you supposed fight with your pants down.

For one, it was too many of them in the small space. Second, Connor had more to lose than he was willing to lose. Some losses are expected in life. Getting raped by eight guys with eight days left before leaving for the halfway house wasn't one of them.

"Mmhm, that's right!" Nate coaxed as Connor sank to his knees in front of him. He closed his eyes as the white boy opened his mouth and leaned in to take the dick. The heat of his breath made his dick throb but the pleasure was not to be. No, this was pure pain when Connor snapped his incisors down on his dick head.

"The fuck!" A young Bando screeched at the sight of the blood. Not louder than Nate who snatched away but not completely. The tip of his dick remained with Connor.

'Tuah!' He spit and hit Nate in the face with his own dick head. "You wanted some head right!"

Nate had his handfuls with a handful of blood. The knife dropped but didn't reach the ground.

"Wanna fuck? Let's fuck! Bwaaaahahahaa!" Connor howled like a raging meth addict, which he was at the moment.

The next closest man got stabbed in his neck and fell away. The next closest man to the door turned and ran. Connor stabbed his way to the door and blocked the others from getting away. The thumps, bumps, thuds and howls turned every head in that direction.

"Let me go put my phone away," someone wisely suggested when a splatter of blood covered the window to the cell.

"Yeah," another agreed since this was going to be more than the daily fights and stabbings of D-Block. People scrambled to put away their contraband before the heat came.

"Uh-oh. Something going on..." The officer announced when she saw the commotion. She looked where everyone was looking and saw the blood covered window. It was time to call a code.

"Lock down!" Sergeant Quick shouted as he led the CERT team into battle. They looked around for anyone resisting so they could beat them into submission. The noise inside Connor's cell came to a sudden stop. All inmate and officer eyes shot up to the door. An eerie silence swept through a space that is rarely ever silent.

The door sounded like an marching army as it crept open. All those eyes just blinked as a man stepped out completely covered in blood, from head to toe. Blood literally dripped from his head and pooled at his feet.

"It's Nasty Nate!" One of the Bandos who escaped cheered. He was relieved to see his partner escape. Nate took a deep breath and coughed up his last. Blood spewed from his mouth and nose before he fell dead.

"Anyone else wanna fuck? Who wants to fuck? Let's fuck!" Connor asked, then demanded. He remembered the treatment from the CERT team upon arrival and decided to fuck them next. He rushed forward but blast from the four tasers subdued the man.

"Clear!" One of the CERT officers announced once they had his wrist and ankles secured. Both wardens were safely outside until he was shackled. He squirmed and bucked but could only hurt himself at this point.

"My god!" Warden Mays exclaimed as she looked over the blood soaked men. Their races couldn't even be determined from all the blood. That was nothing compared to the mess inside the cell. A CERT team member rushed in to clear the cell but rushed out even quicker.

'Argh! Uhhg!' He grunted and groaned as his lunch came back up the same way it went down. Davis just blinked at what could possibly lay ahead in the cell. She had no intentions on looking for herself and gave her sergeant the nod.

"Sergeant Quick," she ordered and nodded ahead. He inhaled, exhaled and marched inside.

Eight men had rushed inside the cell with knives. Two ran, one made it out and died outside. The remaining five looked like they had been ran through a meat grinder. He radioed for medical to come but added a gruesome note.

"No rush," Sergeant Quick advised since dead men aren't in a hurry.

"Call the sheriff," Mays said as she snarled down at Connor. He was fucking with her money and she couldn't sweep a quintuple homicide under the rug.

"Can't call this one a suicide?" Davis wondered and shook her head in reply. He would have to be charged with it. She squinted and leaned in to make out what he was mumbling but couldn't make sense of it.

"Rabbit, rabbit, rabbit," Conner repeated over and over as he vowed revenge. These murders would cost him the rest of his life behind bars and he didn't mind. As long as he got Rabbit. "Rabbit,rabbit, Rabbit season!"

The end.

Stay tuned for The Gentlemen of D-Block 3, Rabbit season.... Coming soon

In the meantime, check out Dolla and Dyme, now available in e-book and paperback...

Dolla and Dyme: Jackin' For Love

A NOVEL BY

Sa'id Salaam

Email: saidmsalaam@gmail.com

Facebook: Free Sa'id Salaam and Black Ink Publications

Cover: Michael Horne

Editor: Tisha Andrews

"Is that him?" Dolla asked, squinting through the dimly lit club. The ice on the target's neck illuminated him, putting him on his radar from all the way across the room. The dancer in front of him looked in the direction he was looking while still popping her caramel ass cheeks in his face.

"He shole look like the one," his equally ambitious partner Dyme said, licking her lips at the tasty lick in front of them. A good lick has a taste, and it's sweet. After wearing a three-thousand-dollar designer outfit and another ten around his neck, they were going to need a shot of insulin after this one. "It sure looks like him."

The mark must have wanted to get robbed when he pulled out a wad of cash and made it rain on the two dancers dancing in front of him. It was mainly ones and fives, but he still wouldn't have been doing it if he wasn't caked the fuck up. He could be charged as an accessory to his own robbery for flossing so hard. His Instagram post could be used against him in a court of law or holding court in the street.

"Yeah that's him, daddy," she purred like she does when her kitty is stroked. He wasn't supposed to be touching it since the club had a no touching policy but it was his pussy, so he would touch it when and where he wanted. "See, if I bust a nut on your hand you gone swear I did you wrong."

"You do and I'm gonna bend you over this table and give you the business. All of it!" he warned and lolled his head back in laughter.

His bright smile contrasted brilliantly against his dark skin and turned heads. The same heads quickly turned back away since Dyme was quick to beat a bitch up over her man. He felt the same way and stopped fondling her when some locals watched him play in her pussy from a few tables over. He used the liquid she leaked to smooth the thick waves on his head since it worked better than Murrays.

"I'm down," she dared and would have done it if he wanted.

Dolla was the first man to treat her right, so she was down for whatever he wanted. What he wanted now was to relieve all the cities clowns of their money.

Dyme was what's known as a fine muthafucka. She stood five foot six inches and had an athletic body, as in an ass as round as a basketball and firm breast the size a regulation soft balls. What set her apart from most of the highly made up strippers was she was naturally pretty. As pretty as she was, she was as rough as a dirt road. Her round face needed little embellishments to turn heads. A little lip-gloss on the thick lips beat all the beat faces in the club. She further drove the value of her vagina up by not tricking with the ballers. Now they chunked bands at her to get her home and fuck. She accepted a few times but they were the ones who got fucked. Fucked out of their money, drugs and jewels that is. Not one lived to tell about it.

Chapter One

"Yo! Yo! That's her B! That's the bitch I was telling you about!" Yayo shouted and pointed when he spotted the same girl from a week ago. Her round, brown ass was jumping and jiggling under a short pair of shorts now just like it did last week. Except last week he was with one of his baby mamas and couldn't pull up. Now he was with his partner Que, so he pulled up and hopped out.

"Silly nigga ," Que said and shook his head. His boss just hopped out an eighty thousand dollar car to talk to some hood rat eating a twenty five cent bag of chips. "Bitch bad though!"

"Ayo, ma! Hole up, shorty!" he said and grabbed her hand. She twirled around and shot him a look that cut like a blade. It didn't draw blood but did get him to let go. "My bad, ma. I'm just tryna meet you."

"Well, you have, so..." she said and twisted her sexy ass away. Dyme had a natural nasty walk just from the proportion of hips to ass, but she did turn it up a little since she was certain he was watching. He was right along with every other male on the block. Old to young, all looked at as she passed by. Even a baby boy spit out his pacifier and gave her a gummy smile.

"Swing and a miss for strike three!" Que teased when he returned empty handed. It was actually a good thing since they had business. Yayo was one of those clowns who thinks with their dick. He would have blown off their drug deal in a heartbeat if he had bagged the girl.

"Yo, bet a hunnid I bag that bitch!" Yayo dared. Que twisted his face up to show what he thought of betting a hundred dollars on some pussy.

"Or, we could go make a hunnid off this deal. How 'bout that?" Que asked.

"Yeah, I guess," he sighed like he'd rather fuck the chick instead of sell a couple of bricks.

"Girl, what Yayo ass talm'bout?" Dyme's cousin April asked when she made it back to the group of girls she hung out with. They called themselves G.M.G for Get Money Girls, but B.A.B was closer to the truth because these were some broke ass broads.

"Same as all the rest of these Brooklyn niggas talking 'bout some sss!" Dyme shot back. She'd been tricked out some pussy a couple of times and wasn't falling for it again.

"Word. I know that's right. Fuck these niggas," they all said even though Yayo had been inside everyone of them. Including April on some late nights, last second backseat action when he caught her coming home from a party.

"Word," Dyme agreed and opened her bag of chips.

She regretted it instantly when every hand extended for a chip. They shared it just like shared blunts and dick.

Yayo didn't give up easily. In fact, he downright stalked the block for weeks on end trying to get the girl. She finally gave him her number and they began to talk and text and 'like' and 'share'. Persistence pays off in any pursuit, especially the pursuit of pussy and Yayo got that pussy.

Weeks of movies, food, weed, cash, and even some much needed outfits did the trick and they ended up inside a swank hotel. Her friends fucked in motels, back seats and even staircases, but Yayo took her to his main house. He set out the champagne, exotic weed and even a new phone inside of a new purse. In return, she set out some good, clean, wet, tight pussy. It wasn't tricking since he swore they were in a relationship now.

"Don't play me," Dyme pouted when Yayo settled on top of her. Her body was ready, but her mind needed a little reassuring.

"Never that. You, my, lady," he assured her with soft kisses as commas. He reached down and rolled on a condom like she insisted. "We are now an us."

"Okay," Dyme said as she gave in and gave it up. She let out a hiss and winced from the pressure when he entered her. She got her breathing together and settled in to enjoy her new man.

"Mmm," Yayo grunted and screwed up his face. She did too, wondering what was wrong since he just got inside of her. Two strokes later, he was moaning and groaning like he was about to cum. "I'm about to cum!"

"Huh?" she asked because that just didn't make any damn sense. He wined and dined her for months and only fucked her for a few seconds. He couldn't even be called a minute man since you have to stay in the pussy for a whole minute. April always said that if a dude bust that quick it's only because a chick got that good-good, wet-wet. It's to be expected, but they will last longer the second go 'round. Could be true but there would be no second.

"Mmm, shit! That was good. I gotta go," Yayo announced and stood. Dyme was already confused by the micro sex but when he pulled out and got up, he wasn't wearing the rubber.

"The fuck, yo?" Dyme demanded when she reached down and felt the slimy semen he deposited in her vagina.

"My bad," Yayo shrugged and got dressed. It was no big deal to him since he always pulled the trick condom act on young chicks. Meanwhile, Dyme was still in shock, trying to figure out what just happened. His "my bad" echoed in her head the whole way back to the hood. She was in her shower still shaking her head at his "my bad".

Yayo was always throwing her a hundred here or a hundred there but the hundred he gave her when he dropped her off at her Aunt Lynn's house seemed tainted. It felt dirty and she would have thrown it away if she didn't need it so damn much. The only thing she could do was cry, so she cried. Cried herself a river in the shower while washing his seeds out of her.

≈

It took a week of unanswered calls and texts before Dyme accepted that she'd been played. It just didn't make sense if he was one of them fuck 'em and duck'em dudes as long as he could beat the pussy up a little bit. He spent all that time, energy, money and good game to fuck for a few seconds.

It took a month to figure out that she was pregnant from the brief encounter. She was the only chick she knew had knocked her up without a calendar and phone records to match up dicks. No question, Yayo impregnated her which made her calls and texts even more urgent. She saw the nigga everyday when he was stalking her but didn't see a trace of him now.

To add insult to injury to her pregnancy, he didn't pay the bill on the phone he gave her so she couldn't even call or text anyone. Now she never saw him at all. Until today that is.

"Hmph! There go that sexy ass Dolla!" April said with gusto when she spotted the hood's most elusive pretty thug. Just a sighting of the dude made every coochie on the stoop throb. Even Chattie and it sent up a puff of funk in the air.

"He a'ight," Dyme was said when she saw Yayo pulled up to go into the bodega ahead of Dolla. She hopped up and made a beeline over to the corner store, almost getting hit by a gypsy cab when she blindly crossed the street.

"Fuck she got going on?" one of the B.A.Bs asked since she didn't even have a quarter for a quarter water.

"I'on know?" April asked but kept a keen eye out to find out. Especially since Dolla was heading to the same store. She wanted to run over and ask if she wanted her to roll his blunt, light it for him and then suck his dick while he smoked it.

Dyme didn't even notice Dolla as she rushed past him and into the store. He noticed her and bit his lip as he watched her fat ass wiggle by. Dyme finally had this nigga Yayo and he was gonna have to tell her something about something. She caught him in the cooler picking up wine coolers.

"Awe, man!" Yayo groaned when he saw her coming.

"Awe, man what?" Dyme shouted on verge of hysteria. All she wanted to do was tell him she was pregnant so he could break bread to pay for the termination. No way would she even entertain the thought of being baby mama number eight.

"I ain't got time for you," he said and stormed off. He saw they had an audience so he had to put on a little, even if it was a lie. "Plus, yo pussy stunk! That's why I ain't come back for seconds!"

A lifetime of unspoken disappointments flooded Dyme's mind and pushed all reasoning aside. That bullshit her own mother pulled, putting her out over some nigga. Living with her shady aunt and ratchet cousin. Having to hang out with the brokest broads in the borough and now her pussy stank! No, that wouldn't do at all. She made sure to keep a nice, clean vagina.

"Ain't got time for me?" she growled and pulled her straight razor as she followed him from the store. She couldn't have stopped herself even if she wanted to. She didn't want to though, so she savagely took a swipe that opened his face from earlobe to his chin. "Got time for stitches?"

"Oh shit !" the whole block shouted. That included Que sitting in Yayo's car, the G.M.Gs sitting on their stoop and Dolla who had just arrived.

"Did you cut me?" Yayo asked mainly from everyone else's reaction since the super sharp blade was almost painless. For a moment, followed by the burn and gush of blood that seemed to explode on his shirt.

Mind your business Dolla, Dolla said to himself. He had a little thing for Dyme but didn't like the company she kept, so he kept that thing to himself.

"Bitch, I'll kill yo' ass!" Yayo shouted with his cheek flapping as he spoke. His teeth and tongue could clearly be seen through the cut. He snatched Dyme completely off her feet and into the air by her throat. Que reached for his door handle to go help her because he didn't like seeing women beat up. Neither did Dolla who was closer.

"Shit!" Dolla fussed at himself when he realized he wasn't going to be able to mind his business. He pulled a pistol from his back and rushed over. Que fell back to watched the show.

"Choke me!" Dolla dared and gave him a backhand smack with the gun that made the block go, "Ooooh!"

Yayo let Dyme go and she stumbled away and coughed in search of her breath. Dolla wasn't done yet, so he shoved the gun in Yayo's mouth until he gagged. Que just shook his head at the spectacle and sat tight.

"Do it," Que heard himself say like most sidekicks will do. Every right hand man wants to be the man instead of the man next to the man.

Dolla felt his finger tightening on the trigger until he was a millisecond away from splatting his brains on the "rest in peace" mural on the wall behind him. Something shook Dolla's head "no" and he left the pressure off the trigger. He pulled the gun out of Yayo's mouth and dismissed him with a swift kick in the seat of his expensive jeans. Que shook his head again as Yayo ran and got into the car.

"Ain't nobody need your help!" Dyme snapped on Dolla instead of thanking him. Her pride was hurt about getting put on blast and almost getting choked out.

"Whatever. Keep ya legs closed and shit like this won't happen," Dolla said and continued on his mission.

Want more? Available on Amazon!

Urban Aesop

ORDER FORM

✉ Urbanaesop@gmail.com

Urban Aesop

Agent's Name: _____

Phone Number: _____   Date: _____

Email Address: _____

PRODUCT NAME	QNT.	PRODUCT NAME	QNT.	PRODUCT NAME	QNT.
The Ladies of D-Block		Ra and Dre		The Dark Prince 2	
The Ladies of D-Block 2		Ra and Dre 2		Love and Hip Hop	
The Ladies of D-Block 3		Ra and Dre 3		Reverend Cash	
The Ladies of D-Block 4		Ra and Dre 4		Dolla and Dyme	
Bad Cop		Ra and Dre 5		Yolo (the lovely little lunatic)	
Bad Cop 2		Malice and Murder		Yolo 2 (murda mami)	
Bad Cop 3		Malice and Murder 2		Yolo 3 (Sun and Shyne)	
Family Drama		Dope Boy		Yolo 4 (diary of a mad woman)	
Family Drama 2		Return Of The Dope Boy		Yolo 5 (til death does us)	
Family Drama 3		Dope Girl		Yolo 6 (Shyne)	
Family Drama 4		Dope Girl 2		Incarcerated Scarfaces	
Rotten Apples		Dope Girl 3		Salty Chicks and Sweet Licks	
Rotten Apples 2		Dope Girl 4		Salty Chicks and Sweet Licks 2	
Rotten Apples 3		Dope Girl 5		Luv in the Club	
Rotten Lil Peaches		Killa, chronicles of a stick up kid		Luv in the Club 2	
Rotten Lil Peaches 2		Killa Season		Luv in the Club 3	
Rotten Lil Peaches 3		Killa Season 2		The Gentlemen of D-Block	
Rotten Lil Peaches 4		Yung Pimping		The Gentlemen of D-Block 2	
Rotten Oranges		The White Girl (chronicles of a junkie)		Secrets of a pastor's wife	
Rotten Oranges 2		The Champ (chronicles of a junkie)		Secrets of a pastor's wife 2	
Rotten Oranges 3		The Preacher's Wife (chronicles of a junkie)		Secrets of a pastor's wife 3	
Love, Lies and Lacefronts		The Dark Prince			

SUB Total	
Vat/Tax	
TOTAL	

Price is $12.99 each
Shipping is $5 for first book. $1 for each additional book

Payment details

Credit/Debit Card:

Name on Card: _____

Credit Card Number: _____

Expiration Date: _____   Signature

CVC Code: _____   Thank you for your Order

Billing Address: _____